STAKEOUT

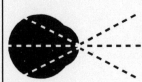

This Large Print Book carries the
Seal of Approval of N.A.V.H.

STAKEOUT

PARNELL HALL

THORNDIKE PRESS
A part of Gale, Cengage Learning

GALE
CENGAGE Learning·

Detroit • New York • San Francisco • New Haven, Conn • Waterville, Maine • London

GALE
CENGAGE Learning®

Copyright © 2013 by Parnell Hall.
A Stanley Hastings Mystery.
Thorndike Press, a part of Gale, Cengage Learning.

LIBRARY OF CONGRESS CATALOGING-IN-PUBLICATION DATA
Hall, Parnell.
Stakeout / by Parnell Hall. — Large Print edition.
pages cm. — (A Stanley Hastings Mystery) (Thorndike Press Large Print Mystery.)
ISBN-13: 978-1-4104-5755-4 (hardcover)
ISBN-10: 1-4104-5755-9 (hardcover)
1. Hastings, Stanley (Fictitious character)—Fiction. 2. Private investigators—New York (State)—New York—Fiction. I. Title.
PS3558.A37327S725 2013
813'.54—dc23   2013001444

Published in 2013 by arrangement with Pegasus Books LLC.

5/13

Printed in the United States of America
1 2 3 4 5 6 7 17 16 15 14 13

For Jim and Franny

1

I staked out the motel.

I love saying that. It's what a tough PI would say. In a book, I mean. Or on TV. It's the thing they always have in the movies to show detective work is boring — the private eye staking out the motel. It makes me laugh, because I'm a private eye, and that's not boring. That's exciting. That's surveillance. I interview accident victims, and photograph cracks in the sidewalk. Compared to which, sitting in a car outside a motel really rocks.

I was on stakeout, and happy to be there. The dame — if this were a 40's noir movie she'd be a dame — came to my office and asked me to tail her husband. At least she said he was her husband — in this business you take nothing for granted. I certainly didn't. I got a retainer and I got it in cash.

The broad was named Julie. When I pressed her for a last name she didn't want to give it. Which was pretty silly. Knowing who *he* was, finding out who *she* was wouldn't be that difficult. Julie had short blonde hair, a little ski-jump nose, and knockers that wouldn't quit. I'm not sure what era that expression's from. And I'm not sure what it means. Knockers that wouldn't quit. As opposed to what? Knockers that *would* quit? *I thought we were getting along great. Then her knockers quit, right in the middle of dinner.*

Anyway, little miss steadfast knockers hired me to tail her husband and see if he was stepping out on her, and I was on the job.

Which was not going well. Not surprising, really. So few of my ventures go well. And I don't think it's me. I think it's just life. I think most ventures are doomed to failure. In the private eye trade, it's the nature of the business. We're attempting to provide an elusive and volatile product. There's so much room for error. Tail her husband to see if he's having an affair. All well and good if he's having one. A fruitless task if he isn't. How long do you keep it up? The answer, of course, is as long as the wife is willing to pay.

I was getting fifty bucks an hour, otherwise I wouldn't have been doing it. I suppose I

8

should have asked for more. For my regular ambulance chasing job I get twenty bucks an hour. Fifty seemed like a whopping increase. A hundred seemed like the impossible dream. I suppose in retrospect it was a possible dream and I should have dreamed it. But the idea of charging somebody a hundred bucks an hour to sit in a car and do nothing just boggled the mind.

So far I'd been staking out the motel for three hours. That was a hundred and fifty bucks for sitting on my keister. A tough job, but someone had to do it, and if anyone was going to get paid for sitting on my keister it ought to be me.

The motel was in Fort Lee, New Jersey, just off Route 4. I'd followed the guy there from Manhattan after work. Julie's husband was an insurance salesman for Aflac. She'd made a face when I asked if he knew the duck. I liked that. It meant at least that part of her story was probably true.

As for the rest of it, I was rapidly losing faith. I mean, three hours and no one's shown up? If the guy was meeting someone, where was she?

I was playing little mind games and trying not to pee. From detective fiction, you probably know that private eyes who stake out motels pee in bottles. What they don't tell you is where they get the bottle. It's not like you were going to look for it on the street, find some homeless man with huge plastic bags of deposit bottles and beat him to the next one. I can't see doing that somehow. Basically, you want your own bottle.

A Gatorade bottle is perfect. Only I don't drink Gatorade, I drink Diet Coke. And you can't pee in a Diet Coke bottle. You can't get your dick in. And if you could, you wouldn't admit it. So a quart Gatorade bottle's the ticket. Only problem is, you can't buy an empty Gatorade bottle, you gotta buy a full one. To get an empty bottle, you gotta drink the Gatorade. Only you don't wanna drink the Gatorade, because it'll make you pee. You have to drink it the day before. Only you don't have it the day before, because you didn't have the job the day before, you just got it today.

I wound up buying a quart of Gatorade and pouring it down the sink.

My cell phone rang.

I flipped it open, said, "I thought I told you not to call me on stakeout."

Alice said, "Stanley?"

"Sorry," I said. "Not funny?"

"Hilarious. Listen, are you about done?"

"I'm not even started."

"What do you mean?"

"I tailed a guy to a motel."

"So?"

"He's there alone."

"This is a guy from Manhattan?"

"Yeah."

"He drove out of town and got a motel room alone?"

"That's right."

"Where's the motel?"

"It's in Ft. Lee."

"New Jersey?"

"Yeah."

"What the hell's he doing in New Jersey?"

"Exactly."

"That's ridiculous."

"Yes, it is."

"No one drives over the bridge to Jersey just to rent a motel room. Why in the world would he do that?"

"That's what I'm being paid to find out."

"How are you finding out?"

"By watching the motel."

"If you sit outside watching the motel all night what will you learn?"

"That he wasn't seeing anyone."

"Then what was he doing?"

"How should I know?"

"Doesn't your client want to know?"

"Yes."

"Then there's only one way to find out."

"What's that?"

"Ask him."

"She doesn't want to ask him. She wants me to find out for her."

"How?"

"By watching the motel."

"You're going around again."

"You're leading me around again. What do you want from me?"

"I want you to do the job and come home."

"Why?"

"We need milk."

"Oh, for Christ's sake."

"What's the matter?'

"You can't go out and buy milk?"

"I could. But if you're coming home anyway."

"I'm not."

"You don't know that. She could show up any minute."

"Who?"

"The woman he's seeing."

"We don't know he's seeing a woman. I gotta get off the phone."

"Why? Is something happening?"

"No."

"I don't understand."

She didn't. I don't know if it's true of all wives, or just mine, but an inability to see that they are driving their husband crazy seems deeply ingrained. Alice is a very bright woman, two steps ahead of me on almost any subject. Does she really not recognize the point at which braindrops start dribbling out my ears and I am incapable of following whatever train of thought she wishes to torment me with?

Anyway, I flipped the cell phone closed, prayed she wouldn't call back. Or if she did it would not be an aggrieved phone call, wanting to know why I hung up on her.

Another hour ticked by. A rather uneventful hour. The only item of note was I managed to fill the Gatorade bottle. I also managed to empty it. There was a storm drain on the corner. While I would have made quite a spectacle of myself standing there peeing into it, I had no problem whatsoever walking over there and pouring the bottle down it. Which was a big relief. I had been wondering what I was going to do if I passed my one quart limit. Which wasn't fair, since I wasn't drinking anything. I mean, the cops in the movies are always drinking coffee, with no adverse effects.

Now and then it occurs to me I'm a private detective. See, in my job chasing ambulances for Rosenberg and Stone I don't get a swelled head. I don't swagger around thinking, gee, I'm a big PI. I just go tripping up the stairs in crack houses in a suit and tie hoping like hell the junkies hanging out in the stairwells aren't going to mug me on the way. And they never do, because they think I'm a cop. But the underlying fear that grips me in such circumstances is enough to remind me rather forcibly that any resemblance between me and a TV detective is coincidental and not to be inferred. Nor is the fact that the case I'm investigating invariably involves someone falling down, breaking a leg, and wanting to sue the city of New York. That kind of takes the glamor out of the job. It's only when I get hired by someone else, not Richard Rosenberg, but some walk-in off the street, a person who has no idea who I am or what I do and doesn't realize they are putting their fate in the hands of someone barely competent to do the job — and I use the phrase *barely competent* generously, allowing for the chance that I might actually do something right — and I wind up doing the type of detective work you see in the movies or read in books. Only then do I get a forbidden thrill out of the fact that, at least for the moment, I'm a goddamned private eye.

This was one of those situations. As I say,

staking out a motel is classic PI schtick. I mean, here I am, sitting on stakeout, waiting for the jane to show. To all intents and purposes, even Sam Spade couldn't be doing a better job. I was, at least for one evening, living the dream.

It didn't help, knowing I had to pick up a quart of milk on the way home.

2

The problem with my wife, and without years of psychoanalysis, I doubt if I could ever come close to understanding the problem with my wife, is that she thinks she's smarter than I am. I don't know where she gets this notion. Unless it's from the fact that she *is* smarter than I am, as anyone who's ever met the two of us can attest. Since she knows she is, she thinks she knows what's best for me. And it's hard to dispute the fact, because she is smarter than I am, and I've never won an argument with her in my life.

At any rate, after bitter experience I've learned that immediately following any conversation with her of any length, it would be wise to analyze what she said, and try to ascertain what nuances had escaped my detection. For, among other things, Alice is a master of the Socratic method, and leaves hints to steer me in the right direction, giving me the opportunity to believe I've come up with the ideas myself.

At any rate, I went over the conversation we just had to see if I'd gotten anything out of it besides milk.

Alice seemed to be gently ridiculing my stakeout. Which I was reluctant to admit, since my stakeout was the only thing that pleased me about the job. And there she was, asking me what I expected to accomplish. When I said ID'ing the woman, she asked me what I expected to accomplish if the woman didn't show up. I said the only way to find out is to ask him, and I said the client doesn't want to ask him. And what did she say then? I couldn't remember, exactly. Whatever it was it bothered me. It bothered me because it was one of those how-can-he-be-so-dumb comments. She was waiting for the penny to drop and me to make the obvious conclusion. All I had to do was figure out what Alice was trying to tell me.

Okay, if the woman never shows up I won't know who she is. Nothing wrong with that statement. Seems perfectly simple and straightforward. Let's break it down. The woman hasn't shown up, so I don't know who she is. That has two parts: the woman hasn't shown up; and I don't know who she is. Of those two statements, *I don't know who she is* was undoubtedly true.

That left *the woman hasn't shown up.*

I whipped out my cell phone, called information, got the phone number of the motel. I called it, got the manager.

"Route 4 Motel."

"Yeah. I want to rent a room."

"That's what we do."

"You got two cabins with adjoining doors?"

"Not at the moment."

"What do you mean by that?"

"They're rented."

"They're all rented?"

"We only have two. One of them, both units are rented, the other one, just one."

"The one they're both rented — they staying together?"

"Why?"

"If they're rented together, they'll leave together."

"Well, they're not. So I can't help you. But we're not the only motel on the strip."

"You're the best."

"Yeah, right," the guy said, and hung up.

So. The motel had units with connecting rooms. If the husband rented one, what was to stop the woman he was seeing from renting the other?

That set up an interesting hypothesis. If the woman had entered the motel room by the elaborate ruse of using the connecting door from an adjoining unit that someone else had rented, then this meeting was more clandestine than your average, run of the mill tryst, in fact, something my client would really want to know. Because what Alice was underlining in her other not-so-veiled advice was that the only way to find out what the guy was doing was for my client to ask him. Which she wasn't going to do. Which should have ended the discussion. So why didn't Alice drop it?

Hell.

My client did not want me to go to her husband's place of business, pretend I was interested in life insurance. She didn't want to do anything that would put him wise to the fact he was being tailed. Then he might get cautious and cancel his rendezvous with the woman. I hadn't done that, and the woman hadn't shown up anyway. That was no longer a concern. The situation had gone to hell. It was up to me to save it.

I got out of my car, slammed the door, crossed the street. Went up the motel driveway to unit seven. I took a breath, banged on the door.

There was no answer.

I banged again.

Still nothing.

I leaned my head against the door.

It swung inward.

Just an inch, but enough to freak me out. The door was open!

I didn't care what motivations, rationalizations, or fear of ridicule might be in play at the moment. I knew one thing for certain. I did not want to open that door.

I whipped a handkerchief out of my pocket, used it to grip the doorknob, pushed the door open.

There was no one there. Not surprising, what with no one opening the door. Still, I had seen the guy go in. He had to be there. Unless he'd climbed out the bathroom window. Or went through the connecting door to the adjoining unit. If he did, he could have walked the hell out of there with a hat down over his eyes and I wouldn't have known it.

What a series of depressing ideas.

That was probably what had happened.

I figured I'd better make sure.

I pushed the door closed with my hand in the handkerchief. The doorknob clicked. I wondered if that meant it was locked. I hadn't turned the doorknob, just pushed in on it, since the door was already open. No matter. It would open from the inside.

I walked around the bed and stopped short.

The body of a man lay faceup on the floor. He'd been shot once at close range. A pillow had been used to muffle the shot. There were bloody feathers adhering to the side of his head.

I took deep breaths, tried not to throw up. If you ever find a dead body, that's a good tip. Throwing up is an amateur move. Cops can get DNA from vomit if you choose to leave, and they'll make fun of you if you choose to stay.

I calmed myself down, got my stomach under control. Took a look at the body.

He certainly looked like the man I'd been following. Of course, that man didn't have a hole in his head.

I hadn't decided if I was getting out of there or not, but before I did, I wanted to make the ID. I knelt down, fished in his pocket for his wallet.

The door was kicked in, and the room filled with cops.

3

They took me to the Major Crimes Unit, chained me to the wall. That's not really as bad as it sounds. I'd been chained to one in Atlantic City, back when I started this job, just around the dawn of recorded time. They hadn't gotten me for murder then. As a precedent, that had to be a very good sign.

A beer-bellied plainclothes cop, whose white shirt threatened to pop a button at the waist, was riding herd over me. Not that he needed to, what with me being chained and all. The guy was actually reading the *New York Post.*

The door opened and a plainclothes detective came in who looked as if he'd been sent over from central casting to play the role of a crooked cop. With my track record for judging character, I figured that probably meant he had a heart of gold.

He snapped his fingers at the fat cop, said, "Okay, Morgan, what we got?"

Morgan flipped open his notebook. "Stanley Hastings, suspicion of murder."

"Who'd he kill?"

"Philip Marston."

Well, that was something. With everything falling apart, it wouldn't have surprised me if the guy turned out to be someone else entirely. But, no, that was the name my client had given me.

"Why'd he kill him?"

"I don't know. You have to ask him."

"How'd he kill him?"

"Shot him."

"Where's the gun?"

Morgan held up a plastic evidence envelope.

My mouth fell open. I hadn't seen a gun at the crime scene, and it hadn't occurred to me there was one.

"He have it on him?"

"No. He kicked it under the bed."

"That's pretty dumb."

Morgan looked at me. "No, he's a smart boy. Probably didn't figure on being arrested. Thought he'd be long gone before the cops came."

"His prints on the gun?"

Morgan shook his head. "He wiped it clean."

I got the impression this was a routine.

The bad cop knew the answers to the questions before he asked them. He and Morgan were playing a little scene in front of the suspect, to rattle him and break down his resistance.

They needn't have bothered. I was born rattled. And my resistance was virtually nonexistent. Of course, if they never asked me a question, I wouldn't have to answer.

The cop who wasn't Morgan stood there looking at me. "Forgive me if I stare. Hardly ever see a killer. Leastwise, not a white one. I wonder what his bag is." He looked at Morgan. "Is he a fag? I bet he's a queer. I bet this was a lover's quarrel gone bad."

Oh, great. I not only got a bad cop, I got a homophobic racist too. And the son of a bitch still hadn't asked me a question. He just kept dancing around, playing his little game. I sat and seethed.

I knew what he was doing. He was frustrating me. He was not letting me talk to make me want to talk. He knew before he even asked I wasn't going to cooperate. I was an out-of-town PI, from New York City, no less, a species regarded somewhere between paramecium and pond scum. So he wanted to soften me up for an interrogation he knew would be like pulling teeth.

"Okay, you're a private eye from New

York. You tailed this guy to a motel, staked it out to see what happened. When nothing happened, you went in and found him dead."

I looked at him in surprise. "How did you know?"

He shrugged. "Unless you shot him, that's what happened. You gonna say you shot him?"

"Hell, no."

"Then that's your story. You know it, I know it. The only one who doesn't know it is Morgan, who's too damn dumb. So if you didn't kill him, it's not your gun, you didn't even know it was there. Unless you shot him and kicked the gun under the bed. But that would be too dumb, even for Morgan."

"Thank you," Morgan said.

"Anyway, if you shot him we could prove you fired the gun with a paraffin test. Unless you wore gloves. You know the problem with that, Morgan?"

"If he wore gloves, where are they?"

"Right. So, let's say, just for the sake of argument, you didn't shoot him. In that case, someone else did. If you were on duty, as a private investigator, watching that unit from the time the guy checked in, while you may be a rather unpromising murder suspect, you sure as hell are a promising wit-

25

ness. You saw the murderer. The arrival and departure of the murderer will be logged into your detective's notes. Along with a thumbnail sketch of the killer.

"So, we looked through your possessions when we brought you in here. We also obtained a warrant, and searched your car. Guess what? No notes. So, you're either the world's worst private detective, or you killed him."

He took a breath. "Now, we could go on, but I'm not big on guessing games, and you're probably not big on sitting there being insulted. What's it gonna be? You have the right to remain silent, but that doesn't mean you have to. What do you have to say for yourself?"

4

I told them everything.

I know, I know, that blows my image as a PI. I was supposed to hold out on the cops, follow the clues myself, solve the case ahead of them. Only in this case there seemed no reason. I'd been hired to find out if my client's husband was cheating. Well, he wasn't, at least, not tonight, and certainly not anymore. My client hadn't hired me to find out who killed him. Granted, he wasn't dead when she did, but even so. There was absolutely no reason to hold anything back, so I didn't.

Not that the cops were the least bit grateful. On the one hand, they despised me for talking. On the other, they didn't believe a word I said.

Bad Cop regarded me with disgust unlikely to have been equaled in the annals of the New Jersey police department.

"You just walked in and found him dead?"

27

"Yes."

"You expect us to believe that?"

"It's what *you* said I did."

"It's what I said your *story* would be. I didn't say it was true."

"I'd have to be the stupidest guy alive to shoot the guy and kick the gun under the bed."

"What's your point?"

"How can you not believe my story?"

"It has a few significant gaps."

"Like what?"

"I'd say the most glaring was the arrival and departure of the killer."

I said nothing.

He continued, "According to your story, no one had an opportunity to kill him except you."

"Not at all."

"What do you mean, not at all?"

"If you searched the motel room, perhaps you noticed the connecting door."

"That was locked."

"Of course it was locked. The killer locked it when he went out."

"How'd the killer get the guy to open the door?"

"Maybe this meeting was part of some prearranged plan."

"The guy planned to be killed? I tend to

doubt that."

"He didn't plan to be killed. He planned to take part in some shady deal. He was sneaking though a connecting door to meet someone in a motel room so they wouldn't be seen entering his."

"Or he wouldn't be seen entering theirs," Morgan said.

Bad Cop looked at him in surprise. "You buy this guy's story?"

"No. But in case it happens to be true, no reason why the dead guy's so all-fired important. Maybe there's a big meeting next door that this guy doesn't want to be known to take part in, so he arranges to rent the next unit so he can be there without being seen entering. As far as I'm concerned, that makes more sense than these guys rented a unit so they could call on him."

"Yeah, fine," Bad Cop said. "But that's only if we buy this guy's story. Which there's no reason to do." He turned back to me. "We searched your car, and you know what we found?"

"Not much."

"Well, we found a Gatorade bottle smelled like piss. I suppose you have some romantic idea guys on stakeout piss in 'em. But we didn't find a gun permit."

"I don't have a gun permit."

"Why don't you have a gun permit?"

"I don't have a gun."

"What the hell kind of PI are you, you don't have a gun?"

"Your basic, law-abiding type."

"Yeah, sure. Now I'll tell you what happened. You followed the guy to a motel where he was shacking up with a hot babe. You phoned the wife, she came racing over, burst in, shot him dead."

"What happened to the hot babe?"

"She went home. She's married, she doesn't want to get involved. That leaves you with the wife. You're freaked, you probably would have split, except she's got a gun. She offers you a ton of money to stake out the place until the police arrive so you can swear she was never there."

"That's not what happened."

"All right. Let's ask her."

The door opened and my client came at me like a harpy from hell. Her hair was a mess, her lipstick was smeared, her eyeliner was running down her cheek. "You son of a bitch!" she screamed, and came flying across the room, an outraged goddess swooping down to disembowel the mortal chained to the stake.

Morgan intercepted her in the nick of time, steered her away. She slumped into

30

his arms, weeping uncontrollably. She twisted from his grasp, backed off, and stood there like a beast at bay, panting, her chest rising and falling in a way that I had to remind myself was not the least bit erotic. This was difficult as she was wearing a tank top not designed to stifle such thoughts.

"You're supposed to be a PI. You're supposed to help people. How could you do it? Oh, my God! My God!"

Bad Cop said, "Just so there's no mistake, ma'am, this is the man you hired?"

"Of course it's him." She looked ready to go across the room again. Morgan took a protective step between us. "I can't believe it. I just can't believe it."

"You hired him to follow your husband?"

"That's right."

"Because you thought he was having an affair?"

"Yes."

"He didn't call you, tell you your husband was at the motel?"

"No, he didn't."

"You didn't try to find your husband at the motel?"

"Of course not."

"This is the first time you've seen him since you hired him?"

"Yes, of course it is. Why are you asking

31

me these questions?' "

"Sorry, ma'am. We just have to keep the record straight. The fact is, you haven't seen him until just now?"

"That's right."

"There now, ma'am. We won't inflict him on you any longer. If you'll just come with me."

Morgan ushered her out. I was glad to see her go. I would have liked to talk to her, but not in front of the cops. Not in her current mood. Good God, what a shock. Yesterday her biggest problem was her husband was stepping out on her. Today he's a corpse.

Bad Cop turned to me. "So, what do you have to say for yourself?"

"I've already said it."

"Do you confirm that's your client?"

"I thought she confirmed it."

"She did."

"Do you dispute it?"

"No, she's my client. At least she was. I have a feeling this may terminate the employment."

Morgan came back in the door.

"How's she doing?"

"Okay. She's sort of mad at him."

"Of course she is. He killed her husband."

"So she says. Of course, she's not a good witness. She couldn't testify to it. Unless she saw him do it."

"I doubt it. Her anger seems genuine. If she watched him do it, why would she be pissed off?"

Morgan shrugged. "Some broads are like that. They ask you to do something, they're angry when you do."

"What's the matter, Morgan. Have a fight with your wife?"

"Leave my wife out of it."

"You're the one always bringing her up."

"I can bring her up. She's my wife."

"You're saying I can't talk about her?"

"You can talk about her when I talk about her. That's friendly. Bringing her up when I don't talk about her is something else."

My head was coming off. They'd forgotten about me. My client's widow had just tried to kill me, and they could have cared less. There was only one reason for that. They'd made up their minds. My client's accusation had cinched it for them, they were going to hold me come hell or high water, and now they were just waiting for some prosecutor or other to show up and haul me in front of a judge.

I wondered if I should call Richard. But it seemed strange to demand an attorney when no one was questioning me. I had to wait till they did. It couldn't be long. They couldn't keep up the small talk forever. It would drive them nuts. It was driving me nuts.

Bad Cop turned back to me. I braced myself, ready to stick up for my rights.

"Okay," he said, "you can go."

I stared at him. "What?"

"We'll bring you back if we need to talk to you some more, but right now we're done."

Morgan was on his feet. Standing he looked portlier than ever. He unlocked the handcuff, ushered me over to a side door. I followed him down a dark corridor into an anteroom where four men in plain clothes were hanging out. I thought they were cops until Morgan said, "Okay, guys, let's go," and I realized they were suspects just like me. Well, not *just* like me. Some of them were probably guilty.

Morgan pushed the door open, and out we went.

It was another dark hallway, so dark the guy behind me kept bumping me into the guy in front of me.

I was just wondering why they didn't turn on the lights when someone did. Suddenly it was so bright I could barely see my hand in front of my face.

A voice said, "Stop moving. Stand straight. Face front."

I stopped, looked around.

Behind me was a white wall with black height markings on it.

I was in a police lineup.

5

I glared at Bad Cop. "I can't believe you did that."

He shrugged. "What do you mean, me? I didn't do anything. You're the killer."

"If you wanted me to take a lineup, all you had to do was ask me to take a lineup. You didn't have to trick me into it under the guise of letting me go."

"What do you mean, 'trick' you into it? No one tricked you into anything. Everything was by the book. We put you in a lineup, and the witness picked you out."

"Picked me out as what?"

"As the killer, of course."

"Yeah, right," I scoffed. "You got an eyewitness saw me pull the trigger."

"Are you worried we do?"

"I'm not worried at all, because I know you don't."

"We've got the next best thing."

"What's that?"

36

"Eyewitness evidence *and* circumstantial evidence. You put the two together it makes quite a convincing case."

"Yeah, well I'm not convinced. You gonna let me go, or do I have to call my attorney?"

"You have the right to an attorney. You always *have* had the right to an attorney, and you always *will* have the right to an attorney. He's not going to do you any good, since we got you dead to rights on a murder rap, but you certainly have the right to one."

"I want to call my attorney."

"Your request is duly noted. We'll be sure to accommodate you at our earliest convenience."

Bad Cop went out the door and returned moments later ushering in a twitchy-nosed gentleman who looked not at all happy to be there.

"Is that the guy?" Bad Cop demanded.

I stared at him. Since I didn't know who "the guy" was, I had no idea if the twitchy-nosed gentleman was him.

It turned out he wasn't talking to me.

Twitchy-nose was a little man with a whiny voice. "You said I wouldn't have to meet him," he complained.

"Oh, come on. He's handcuffed to the wall."

"Now he is," Twitchy-nose whined. "What

about later?"

"There's not going to be any later, if we get him for murder."

He shuddered. "Yeah, murder. You got me face-to-face with a killer."

"So. This is the guy you saw?"

"I don't like this."

"The quicker you get through it, the quicker you'll be out of here."

"Yeah, that's him."

"What did he do?"

"Walked across the parking lot, knocked on the door of unit seven."

"What happened then?"

"Someone opened the door and let him in."

6

Richard Rosenberg was at his scathing best, and, trust me, that's good. Richard didn't get to be New York City's top negligence lawyer by being polite. His withering sarcasm in court could bring opposing counsel to their knees. Attorneys settled out of court with Richard just so they didn't have to meet him in court. His settlements were proportionally higher than those of any other negligence lawyer, and deservedly so.

"You are the stupidest private investigator who ever walked the face of the earth."

"Richard —"

"You are the stupidest *person* who ever walked the face of the earth. You get arrested for murder. So, do you call your lawyer? No. You tell the cops everything."

"Because I had nothing to hide."

"Why do you have nothing to hide?"

"Because I didn't *do* anything."

"And you *know* that an innocent person

could never be convicted of anything. Couldn't happen. It would offend your romantic ideas of right and wrong."

"I didn't think this would happen."

"You didn't think this would happen." He rolled his eyes and shook his head. "Well, that makes it all right then. It's not your fault, because you didn't expect it to happen."

Richard swung into lecture mode. "If a guy gets arrested for murder, there are basically two things he can do. One, he can shut the hell up and call his lawyer. That is the preferred method. That is the one all lawyers instruct their clients to employ. That is the one the cops are required to suggest. It's shocking, what an unappealing option they make it out to be. It's even more shocking that some morons fall for that line."

"Richard —"

"But that's method one. Two, the non-preferred method, the less-desirable method, the method where suspects invariably trip themselves up, is to try to talk their way out of it. To tell a story, which, if true, would mean they couldn't possibly have done it.

"Then there's the third method — well, it's not really the third method, no one's ever used it, I think you've just invented it

— the third method, which is so mind-numbingly stupid it defies comprehension, is to tell a story that, if true, not only means you could have done it, but proves you were *the only person in the world* who could have done it." Richard shook his head. "I don't know why more suspects haven't come up with that strategy yet, but for some reason they haven't. I'm really impressed with you for thinking of it."

"Any time you're through beating me up."

"Beating *you* up? Hey, it's not like I haven't defended you from a murder charge before. I guess that was too easy. I guess I didn't impress you. I guess it looked like I was hardly working. So, you decided to up the stakes. Give me a bit of a challenge. Make it worth my while."

" 'Keep you on your toes' was the cliché I was going for."

"So, you not only talked, you took part in a lineup."

"I was tricked into it."

"Sure, sure. You thought you were going to the men's room. By the time you realized there weren't any urinals it was too late."

"They told me I was going home."

"You always go home in a line?"

"You had to be there."

"Yes, I did. If my client had called me, I

41

would have been."

"We've covered that."

"So, the guy picked you out of a lineup as the guy he saw go into the unit."

"He's wrong."

"Oh, he didn't see you go into the unit?"

"No, he saw me go in. He's wrong about how I did it."

"I understand. You went in strong and manly, he says like a chickenshit."

"No, he says the guy opened the door for me."

"What!?"

"I knocked on the door. It was ajar. I called out, couldn't hear any answer. Pushed it open."

"This guy claims it was opened from inside?"

"That's right."

"Did you touch the knob?"

"No."

"Too bad."

"Why is that too bad."

"I could argue you opened the door."

"I didn't *have* to open the door. It was already open."

"There's no need to get testy."

"You're blaming me for something I didn't do."

"Like calling me?"

"Richard —"

"This motel manager's a problem. Undoubtedly the guy's a total asshole who's going to stick to his story no matter what. It would be nice if I had *something* to argue."

"How about the truth?"

Richard made a face. "Only incompetents argue the truth. The truth shall set you free? What bullshit. Rely on the truth, you can kiss your ass goodbye. I mean, look at the motel manager. He's going to say the guy opened the door for you. Is that true? Not according to you. But does that matter? If I can't shake his story, you're going down."

"Can you shake his story?"

"I don't know, I haven't heard it yet. Ten to one he's an opinionated cuss who's going to dig in his heels and stick to his guns. Not that it matters. The way you tell it, you're the only one who could have done it."

"That's not true."

"Oh? How is that?"

I gave him the connecting door theory. I can't say he was terribly impressed.

"So, I not only gotta argue that the manager's mistaken, I gotta argue that some guy from the adjoining unit, who you didn't happened to see enter or leave, slipped next door and killed him after he conveniently rented the adjoining unit and left the con-

43

necting door unlocked. What an extraordinary stroke of luck for the killer."

"It wasn't luck. They were in cahoots."

"Cahoots? Did you just use the word 'cahoots'? I hope you don't expect me to use it in court." He shook his head. "What a pain in the ass. Drag me over to Jersey, put me in a no-win situation."

"Sorry my murder charge inconvenienced you," I said dryly.

"Well, there's no help for it. You've been ID'd." Richard cocked his head at me. "And you know what that stands for."

"No. What?"

"Incredibly dorked."

7

They dragged me before a judge who arraigned me for murder, and set bail at a million dollars. I was flattered to be valued so highly, but I didn't happen to have a million on me. Richard fought like a tiger, but it was a capital charge, and I was from out of state. The best he could get him down to was two hundred and fifty thousand. It might as well have been a billion. I couldn't raise it.

They took me out and locked me in a cell.

Morgan was back a half hour later. "All right, let's go."

"I'm not talking without my attorney."

"Little late for that."

Morgan unlocked the cell, hauled me out.

"I've hired an attorney. I've been arraigned. Any attempt to talk to me now is interfering with my rights. I have nothing to say. I want to go back to jail."

"Sorry."

"What?"

"Can't help you."

"Then you better help yourself. When my attorney gets you on the stand and grills you about this conversation, how do you think that's going to look?"

"I imagine it's going to be pretty embarrassing," Morgan said, but he didn't break stride.

He dragged me out into the booking room.

Richard was waiting.

"Here you go," Morgan said. "He's all yours. Just between you and me, I think there's something wrong with him. Didn't want to be released." He shrugged and walked off.

"Get your things," Richard said. "We're going home."

I stared at him. "What the hell happened?"

"I bailed you out."

My mouth fell open. "You put up two hundred and fifty thousand dollars?"

"It's a bail bond."

"You got a bail bond?"

"Well, I wasn't going to put up a quarter of a million cash. That would be pretty stupid."

"How much is a bond?"

"Ten percent."

"You put up twenty-five?"

"How you gonna work for me if you're in jail?"

"You know how many cases I'd have to handle to make twenty-five thousand dollars?"

"Not that many, actually. Oh, you mean your salary. We're not talking about that. The point is getting you released."

"How did that become the point?"

Richard frowned. "Let's get out of here."

I signed for my valuables, such as they are, put my wallet and watch and an embarrassingly paltry amount of money in my pockets, and followed Richard outside.

We were in a small New Jersey suburb, indistinguishable from any other small New Jersey suburb, bounded only by the invisible lines that separated designations such as Ft. Lee, Teaneck, Englewood, and the like.

"Where's your car?"

"Surely you jest," Richard said. "I took a car service."

"Where's your car service?"

"They're on speed dial. I'll call them in a minute. Right now we need to have a little talk."

"Uh, oh."

"Hey, it isn't every pro bono lawyer posts bail. You could at least listen."

"I'm listening."

"Okay, look, we got a problem. You framed yourself for murder. Usually a poor move, but with your track record, not impossible. Complicating things is the testimony of the motel manager."

"I don't need a recap, Richard. What's the bottom line?"

"Twenty-five grand and you're impatient?"

"Are you going to work the phrase 'twenty-five grand' into every conversation?"

"Not when I get it *back*. I get it back when you go to jail or we clear your name. Going to jail could be a long process, what with trials, appeals, and what have you. So clearing your name is the way we want to go. I am somewhat hamstrung at this juncture. There's not much I can do until the trial, which, as I say, could be a while. Even then, the outcome is in doubt."

"Excuse me?"

"The motel manager's an obstinate jerk. I can make him look like an obstinate jerk, but I can't make him retract his story, and if the jury buys it you're toast."

I stared at him. "That's why you got me out?"

"That's right. You have to solve the crime."

8

Alice was predictably supportive. "You didn't do anything wrong."

I felt like shit. Alice has the ability to support me wholeheartedly while totally undermining my position, leaving me like a cartoon character who's walked off a cliff and suddenly realizes he's standing in midair.

"What do you mean, I didn't do anything wrong? I found a dead body and got arrested."

"Well, you shouldn't have done that."

"Then I did something wrong."

"No, you didn't."

"Are you saying I *should* get arrested for murder?"

"Now you're just being silly."

That's why I can't argue with Alice. Every time I win a point she tells me I'm being silly. Which is unfair. You can be silly and still win a point. I wondered if I should tell her that. I was sure she'd have a comeback.

"Don't worry about it," Alice said. "Richard will handle things."

"Richard *won't* handle things. Richard got me out of jail because he realized he can't handle things."

"No he didn't."

"He *told* me so."

"Yes, but he's a lawyer. They'll tell people anything."

"He's my lawyer. And he's very concerned."

"I don't think so."

"He is. That's why he got me out of jail."

"Don't be silly. He's handling a murder case. He got you out of jail to do his legwork."

"That's ridiculous. He could just hire someone."

"He'd have to pay him."

"He has to pay me."

"Twenty bucks an hour. He's not going to find anyone else that cheap."

"Oh, give me a break. It cost him twenty-five thousand dollars to get me out."

"Yes, but he'll get it back, won't he?"

"Eventually."

"Yeah, but he will, and then all he'll be out is the twenty bucks an hour he paid you. As opposed to someone else who's gonna cost him a thousand bucks a day."

"A thousand?"

"Say five hundred. Your eight-hour day's 160. Still a huge saving."

"Richard's not that cheap."

"Oh, really?"

"Well, maybe he is that cheap, but that's not why he did it."

Alice put her hand on my shoulder. Smiled. "Stanley, if it makes you feel better to think that Richard, with twenty years' experience and what I understand is a rather impressive track record in court, feels that you, an unemployed actor/writer permanently moonlighting as an ambulance chaser, are more qualified to mount a first-degree murder defense, then go ahead and think that."

"I think it's only first-degree if you kill a cop."

"Is that true?"

"I don't know. I'd have to look it up."

"Never mind. It'll be on the Internet."

And Alice was off to the computer, leaving me even more unsettled than before the conversation had begun.

9

Early next morning I drove out to the motel and pulled up in front of the manager's office.

He wasn't glad to see me. He kept the counter between us, looked prepared to duck. "Hey, this is not my fault. I'm sorry I saw you, but I saw you. That's my job. A guy rents a unit, a girl shows up, that's fine. Another guy shows up, that's trouble. If you'd busted in the door, I'd have called the cops. It was a relief when he let you in."

"He didn't let me in."

"I don't want to get into it. Hell, I shouldn't be talking to you at all."

"Right. I don't care about that. That's your opinion, and you're welcome to it."

He looked at me suspiciously. "I am?"

"I'm not here to make trouble, honest. I'm just trying to find out what happened."

He looked at me as if I told him I knew tomorrow's lottery numbers. "Uh huh."

"I'm just wondering. The man in the room. The man they say I killed. How was he registered?"

"How was he registered?"

"Yeah. When he signed the register. Did he use his own name?"

"Why?"

"I'm trying to make sense out of this. It doesn't make sense to me. If I knew what name he was registered under, it might be a clue."

"If I had a clue, I would give it to the police. I would not give it to you. No offense."

"None taken. You gotta live here. You got a job. Just anything you could do to help me out without interfering with your relationship with the police department would be appreciated."

Appreciated was the wrong word. I knew it the minute it was out of my mouth. I could see him latch onto it.

"Yeah, well if the police knew I was talking to you, that would *not* be appreciated. All you're going to do is get me into trouble. Get out of here or I'll tell the cops. Isn't there some law about harassing a witness? I don't wanna make trouble for you, but I don't want you to make trouble for me."

I didn't want him calling the cops. I got

54

the hell out of there.

I must say I took his desire not to make trouble for me with a grain of salt. His eyewitness account was enough to get me convicted of murder. I wondered what his idea of making trouble was.

10

"I hear you got arrested for murder."

"That's right."

"Did you do it?"

"Fuck you."

MacAullif leaned back in his desk chair, and cocked his head. The chair squeaked in protest. A big man to begin with, the sergeant had put on a little weight lately.

"I'm not familiar with that plea. Innocent, guilty, even nolo contendere. That I know. But fuck you? That's a new one on me."

"You're in an awfully good mood."

"Well, you're in trouble. That's always entertaining."

"Usually it pisses you off."

"Yeah. But it's in Jersey. Outside my jurisdiction. There's nothing I can do."

"Well, actually. . . ."

"Well, actually." MacAullif shook his head. "Count on the dickhead to rain on my parade with a 'well actually.' "

"You must know New Jersey cops."

"Apparently not as many as you."

"Do you know Sergeant Fuller of the Major Crimes Unit?"

"No. Why?"

"My arresting officer."

"God help him. I was your arresting officer once. Look what it got me."

"Know anyone you could ask?"

"Why?"

"Guy's all over my case. First I thought he and his partner were playing good-cop, bad-cop, now I think he *is* Bad Cop. I'd like to know if it's personal, or if he's just doing a job."

"Why'd they pick you up?"

"They found me in a motel room with the corpse."

"Holding the murder weapon?"

"It was under the bed."

"Have your fingerprints on it?"

"No."

"You sure of that?"

"I never touched it. I didn't know it was there."

"Is it possible you touched a gun under some other circumstances which just happened to turn out to be this one?"

I stared at him. "What kind of a hokey conspiracy theory are you dreaming up?"

He shrugged. "I know the way your mind works. If there's an improbable, unlikely scenario, you'll go for it."

"I have not touched a gun within recent memory."

"How's your Alzheimer's?"

"I would remember a gun. Let's not get hung up on the murder weapon. That's just an unfortunate circumstance."

"Like the corpse. What's your connection to him?"

"His wife hired me to tail him."

"Sealing his death warrant. What's the wife like?"

"Perfectly nice."

"She got big tits?"

"What's that got to do with it?"

"I know you. You have a permanent midlife crisis. Let a hot babe walk into your office and your brain turns to Jell-O."

"The wife has nothing to do with this."

"Schmuck. The wife has everything to do with this. She hired you. She gave you the assignment. She's the reason you went to Jersey. Any chance she could have killed him?"

"No."

"I'll take that for a yes. As far as I'm concerned, the wife is guilty until proven innocent."

"She couldn't have done it."

"Why not?"

"I was watching the motel room. She never went in."

"Who did?"

"No one."

"Then he's still alive. Unless he shot himself. Any chance he did?"

"Not unless he didn't want the crime scene to seem cluttered so he slid the gun under the bed."

MacAullif shook his head. "I gotta tell you. If I was a New Jersey cop, you'd look pretty good to me."

"I didn't do it."

"Can you prove it?"

"I don't have to prove I didn't do it. They have to prove I did."

"That's fine in theory."

"What do you mean in theory?"

"The facts you told me prove you did it. So you do have to prove you didn't."

"No, I just have to raise reasonable doubt."

"Good lord, has it come to that?" He shook his head. "What a sad state of affairs. I assume the ambulance chaser's in charge of that?"

"Yeah, but he's not happy."

"Why not?"

I told him about the motel manager.

"So he's lying?"

"Or just mistaken."

"Hell of a mistake."

"Yeah."

"Did he call the cops?"

"Why?"

"Someone did. If it was him, it's good."

"Why is that?"

"He claims the dead guy opened the door and let you in, right?"

"Yeah."

"If that's true, why'd he call the cops?"

"Good point. There'd be no reason."

"There's something you can hit him with. Why'd he call the cops if he thought the guy let you in? So how'd this murder take place? According to you, it couldn't have happened."

I told him about the connecting door.

"Oh, wonderful. The old adjoining room theory. You know how much credence the cops are going to give that?"

"They're not."

"No shit. They got the killer dead to rights. You think they're going to waste time with something that undermines the theory?"

"Of course not."

"That's why you gotta do it."

"Do what?"

"Check it out."

"I can't check it out. The motel manager thinks I'm a killer."

"It is inconvenient being a murder suspect."

"But you could check it out."

"Oh, for Christ's sake."

"Why not? No one thinks *you're* a killer."

"Because I don't do stupid things like that."

"So he doesn't know you from Adam. You could walk in, take a look at his ledger."

"I can't do that."

"Why not? You're a cop."

"I got no jurisdiction in Jersey."

I smiled. "He doesn't know that."

11

MacAullif parked down the block not that far from where I'd been pissing in my Gatorade bottle. I figured that was probably a poor thing to point out. I sat in the police car, waited while he went in.

He didn't come out. I'm sitting there, waiting for something to happen, and nothing did.

I started getting punchy, thinking maybe the guy called the cops. That was stupid. He's talking to a cop, he's gonna call the cops? I mean, the motel manager didn't strike me as someone who's going to cross-examine MacAullif on his authority, wrestle his badge away from him, accuse him of being from New York.

I got more punchy. It occurred to me maybe *I* should call the cops, get them to pick up MacAullif. That'd show him, after lecturing me about getting arrested, claiming it had never happened to him. Though he might have said "arrested for murder." I couldn't recall the details. I was sure MacAullif could.

Before I could opt for such idiocy, MacAullif came out the door. He hopped in the car and we took off.

"Any luck?" I said.

"No. I was in there pricing motel rooms in case I ever want to hang out in this hell hole."

"Did he believe you were a cop?"

"I *am* a cop. I got the guy's undying gratitude for not busting him." He reached in his jacket pocket, pulled out a piece of paper, handed it over.

"What's this?"

"Photocopy of the register. At least the page you want. It's got the dead guy, and the guy next door."

"Really? What's his name?" I looked at the photocopy. "Oh, shit."

"Yeah," MacAullif said. "John Smith. You think there's any chance that might be an alias?"

"Did he remember him?"

"No, he did not. Nor did he remember any of the other John Smiths who checked in all week."

"Damn."

MacAullif reached in his pocket again.

"On the other hand, this might be of more use."

"What's that?"

"Photocopy of the credit card receipt. A lot of John Smiths don't think of that. Sign a phony name on the register, but then don't bother to pay cash. You know how many women get divorced just on the strength of the credit card bill? It's astounding."

"Son of a bitch."

I had MacAullif drop me at my office. I didn't want him to know what I was going to do next.

12

My client couldn't believe I was there. "How dare you!" she said. "How dare you!"

I held up my finger. "Well, think about it. Do I want to be here talking to you? No, I do not. I've been arraigned for killing your husband. You probably think I did it. This is the last place in the world I'd want to be. I don't know who killed your husband. It wasn't me, but the cops think it was, so they're not looking for anyone else. That means I gotta find the killer if I don't wanna take the fall."

I leaned in. "I don't know what the cops told you, but if it's like they told me, I'm the only one who could have possibly done it. Did they tell you about the connecting door?"

"Yes."

That took the wind out of my sails. It was the first rise I'd gotten out of her, but it wasn't the answer I wanted. The way I saw it, the cops wouldn't have even mentioned the door.

I blinked at her stupidly. "They did?"

"Yes. They said you told them some fairy story about how the killer came from another unit, but it was a really stupid idea and no one was buying it."

"It may be a stupid idea, but it must have happened. The guy didn't kill himself."

Her face contorted.

"Sorry. I know. He was your husband. All right, look. Here's the deal. I'm trying to find out who killed your husband. If I can, and I can prove it, I wanna get paid."

She stared at me. "What?"

"You hired me and this is the result. None of it is my fault. From what you told me, I had every reason to expect your husband was going to meet a young woman in that motel room. The fact that that didn't happen was your mistake, not mine. As far as I'm concerned, I'm still on the job. If I can't prove who was shackin' up with your husband, I'm gonna prove who killed him. If I can, I wanna be paid. And I would think you'd wanna pay me."

She stared at me for a long moment. I thought she was softening.

Ever get tired of being wrong?

"Get out!"

13

My car was on a meter on the corner of Madison Avenue and Eighty-fifth. I sat in it wondering what the hell I was going to do.

A car pulled up next to me and honked. The driver pointed, asking if I was going out. I was, but I just wanted to sit for a minute. I didn't want to roll down my window and have the guy roll down his window and tell him that, and have him sitting there watching me for the minute I wanted to be alone with my thoughts, and I didn't have the heart to refuse him the space when I was actually going out. Besides, if I did, within seconds someone else would pull up and honk. So I made the guy's day by nodding yes and starting my car.

I pulled out and managed to get three blocks up Madison before my cell phone rang.

Only three people have that number: Alice, MacAullif, and Richard. Even the switchboard girls don't have it. If they want me, they beep me, same as ever, and I call them. So a call on my cell phone's gotta be something important.

You know, like milk.

I pulled up next to a fire plug to answer the phone. I don't text-message and drive. I wouldn't, even if I knew how.

I flipped the phone open. "Hello?"

It was MacAullif.

"The guy who rented the motel room is Vinnie Carbone, a low-level mobster from the Jersey Shore."

"You're kidding!"

"No."

"Then what's he doing in a Jersey motel?"

"There's no proof he was. The guy rented the room, signed the register John Smith, used his credit card like a schmuck. It doesn't mean he ever set foot in the place, and odds are he didn't. Like I say, he's low level. The type of guy who rents the room, gives the key to someone else. Someone who doesn't want to be seen renting a room. That person uses the motel room and no one is the wiser."

"How do you know all this?"

"I don't, but it figures. The guy's got no reason to rent a room. He's single, has his own digs. If he wants to have an orgy, who's to stop him? On the other hand, if some married big shot Vinnie Carbone reports to wants to have a discreet little fling, well what better place than a motel room he has no connection with whatsoever?"

"Someone could see his car parked in front of it."

"Yeah. And the bluebird of paradise could shit on your head, but that don't mean it's going to happen. Did *you* notice a car parked in front of the unit?"

"That's not the point."

"There you are. The guy could risk no one seeing his car more than he could risk walking into the motel manager's office, signing his name, and letting the guy get a look at his face and a scan of his credit card. Which doesn't mean it happened. This schmuck Vinnie could have rented the motel room just so he could go next door and knock off your client's husband. I'm not sure why he would do such a thing."

"You think the big shot he's working for might do such a thing?"

"Big shots have more to lose than small shots. Again, I'm not saying it happened. How long were you watching the motel?"

"What's that got to do with it?"

"It was several hours, right?"

"Yeah. So?"

"The thing about a stakeout job is it's boring. Staring at the same thing for hours. Your eyes glaze over. You nod out, don't even know you did it."

"I didn't nod out."

"Hey, don't get so huffy. I'm not saying you're a bad PI. I'm saying you're mortal. You fell asleep, maybe it hurts the exalted image you have of yourself as a fearless private investigator, but it's a damn sight better than being convicted of murder. As I'm sure your attorney will advise."

"Are you saying Richard is going to tell me to say I fell asleep?"

"No. He's gonna say you got bored with surveillance so you killed the guy just to liven things up. You gotta understand you're talking lawyers, theories, reasonable doubt. Doesn't have to have happened. You just gotta show it *could* have happened."

"It didn't happen."

"You, of course, take a moral stand and cheerily march off to jail, rather than even *suggest* an untruth."

"So who's the big shot? Who'd Vinnie work for?"

"I don't know."

"You didn't ask?"

"Hell, no. And I'm not gonna, either. I want nothing to do with the case. I pulled his rap sheet, so I know he's connected. I can do that without seeming like I'm interested. But I'm not asking any questions."

"You got an address on Vinnie?"

"Yes, I do. If I give it to you just to get you off the phone, will you try to stay out of trouble?"

"I'm not going to get in trouble."

"You're already in trouble. I mean stay out of any more."

"Just give me the address."

He did. I copied it into my notebook, slipped the cell phone back in my pocket, and headed for the Jersey Shore.

14

I don't watch the show. I know there's a Snooki and a Situation. Or maybe that's *Real Housewives.* Or *Desperate Jersey Wives.* Or some equally improbable concept the public inexplicably likes. To me the Jersey Shore always reminded me of beaches. Not the movie, which I also haven't seen, but the sand with the ocean attached. Riding the waves is one of my favorite occupations. I used to do it with my son Tommie. Now I generally do it alone. But I don't get to do it that often. Throw the word "shore" into an assignment and my interest picks up immensely.

Not this time. Vinnie Carbone may have been involved with the Jersey Shore mob, but he lived in a suburb of Elizabeth. When I found the guy's house it was as far away from the ocean as one could imagine. In fact, you wouldn't have even known there was a shore involved. He lived on a grungy street of modest dwellings, further proof that Vinnie Carbone was not high up on the food chain. Vinnie's house was a two-story affair painted a shocking but dirty pink, faded, and in ill repair. It was stark with no visible amenities, with the exception of a garage, the door of which was closed. Naturally. The guy could have had no garage or a garage with the door open. Then at least I would have known if he was home. But, no, the son of a bitch had to have a garage with the door closed, so there was no way to know if he was home or not.

What am I saying? I'm a PI. I can do these things.

I whipped out my cell phone, called information, asked if they had a listing for Vinnie Carbone at that location. Sure enough, they did. I wrote the number in my book, broke the connection, punched it in.

The phone rang six times, then an answering machine picked up. "I'm not in. Leave a message, I'll get back to you."

The voice sounded terse, frustrated, sulky almost. I could imagine the guy had some sort of wise-ass voice message he thought was hysterically funny, only some of the big boys didn't think so, and told him to change it.

I hung up the phone, contemplated my

next move. It was disappointing the guy wasn't home. I'd planned on following him up the food chain to see who he worked for, but you couldn't follow a guy who wasn't there. It was a little counterproductive to stake out an empty house. If MacAullif found out, his sarcasm would reach new heights.

Of course, if I didn't, the guy would come driving up five minutes after I left, and I'd never know it.

So what did I do? Go home and keep calling his phone until I got an answer? That would be a bitch if he had caller ID. He could trace me and kill me.

Shit!

Could he trace me from the hang-up?

I didn't think so, but I've been wrong before. Alice could point to the occasions.

If I remembered correctly, our caller ID has lists of all the phone calls that had come in, so you could look back and see what they were. Could you delete from that file? I wasn't sure, but I thought you could. Surely you wouldn't have to carry them forever. And if you could, it must be very simple to do, or jerks like me couldn't do it.

And Vinnie Carbone wasn't home.

I wondered if he left his door open. In a suburban setting, people didn't always leave their doors locked. Of course, most people weren't in the mob, but still. Wise guys would have a sense of entitlement, of power, a feeling they were invincible. Even low-level wise guys like Vinnie. *Especially* low-level wise guys like Vinnie. That sense of entitlement was what it was all about. He might have even left the front door un-locked. I could get in there, delete my cell phone number from the tape.

The only thing stopping me was MacAul-lif's warning not to get into trouble. I'd said I wouldn't. That wasn't a lie. I had no inten-tion of getting into trouble. But I hadn't promised to do absolutely nothing to make *sure* I didn't get into trouble. I'd just basi-cally promised to be careful. I mean, what's the worst that could happen?

Well, he comes home, catches me, and shoots me.

That was a bit of a deterrent. But what was the likelihood? He'd have to put his car away in the garage, and I'd hear the garage door.

Or he wouldn't. I don't know that he parks in the garage, I'm just assuming he does, but he may not use the garage at all. He could just park in the driveway. And the only reason I don't know that is because he isn't home.

That started a train of thought. Could I recognize car tracks in the driveway? If so, could I tell whether a car had been parked there or merely driven straight into the garage? Well, certainly not from where I was staked out in my car. I'd have to get out, cross the road, check it out.

And leave my car parked where?

Right where it is.

Where anyone could see it.

But who would be looking? And why would they care?

It told myself for the umpteenth time that I was in the wrong line of work. Unfortunately, I'd never learned any other.

I got out of my car, crossed the road.

If there was a message in Vinnie's driveway, I didn't get it. Not only couldn't I tell if car tracks led into the garage, I couldn't even tell if there were any car tracks at all.

I began a succession of increasingly stupid moves, beginning with seeing if the garage door was locked.

It was.

Then was the door to the breezeway locked?

It was.

Was the front door locked?

It was.

Was there any reason to continue circling

the house?

Only that it would keep me from going bonkers in the car.

I continued around the house. A back window looked promising, but wasn't.

The kitchen door clicked open.

What?

How did a low-level mobster live this long, he doesn't even lock his door?

It occurred to me it would be a really good time to get out of there.

Right after I erased my number from caller ID.

I pushed the door open, stepped into the kitchen. I was lucky in that it wasn't dark out yet, I didn't have to risk a light.

All right, where's the phone, where's the answering machine, where's the caller ID?

There was a phone on the kitchen wall, but there was nothing attached. That wasn't the one I wanted. There would be an extension in the office or the living room.

I hoped I wouldn't have to go into the bedroom upstairs. A bad place to be when you hear a car. I'm way too old for jumping out of upstairs windows. Which is not as depressing as it sounds. I was never young enough for jumping out of bedroom windows.

The door from the kitchen led into a small

living room with couch, chairs, TV, and a coffee table littered with racing forms. Nothing to indicate Vinnie was the type of swinger who liked to hang out in cheap motels. Which indicated, as MacAullif had suggested, that in all likelihood he had not rented the room for himself.

This was all very interesting, but there was no phone. How'd the guy get along without a phone? He must use his cell phone and —

Jesus!

Could I have *called* his cell phone?

Then there'd be no way to erase it. It would be in his pocket. He could be looking at it right now. It would say Missed Call, just like mine did when someone failed to leave a message. And he'd press it and it would give him my phone number. And he'd trace it and find out who I was. He could even call me and —

My cell phone rang and I nearly peed my pants.

And me without a Gatorade bottle.

Jesus Christ, where the hell was it? Jacket pocket. Pants pocket. Why can't I be consistent? I can never find the damn phone. It'll keep ringing and ringing. Until it stops. Then it will say Missed Call.

No it won't. It will go to voice mail. I do not want this guy's voice on my answering machine.

Now I really *do* have to pee.

I whipped it out — my cell phone — and flipped it open.

"Stanley. Where are you?"

"Not a good time, Alice."

"Why? Are you driving?"

"Not at the moment."

"The office called. You're not answering your beeper."

I certainly wasn't. I'd put it on silent before I called on the widow and never turned it back on.

"Sorry, I'll call 'em," I said, but I didn't. I hate business calls when I'm breaking and entering.

I put the phone on mute, continued my hasty inspection of the house.

I completed my search of the downstairs, found nothing. The phone in the kitchen was it.

It looked like I'd have to go upstairs after all.

I went up a flight of straight and narrow stairs. I figured using them was the only time Vinnie walked the straight and narrow. Realized that was very bad and I was getting punchy. Where's the damn phone?

There were three bedrooms and a bathroom on the landing.

There was no phone in the first bedroom.

There was no phone in the second bedroom.

There was a phone in the third bedroom, but I didn't use it to check the caller ID.

Instead I stared at the body on the floor that I assumed was Vinnie Carbone.

15

He'd been shot at close range. At least, close enough to hit him in the head. The bullet appeared to have shattered his right cheekbone just below his eye. I say "appeared" to allow that my assumption might have been wrong. Long years of living with Alice have taught me that.

The man was thin and wiry with dark, curly hair. He had sideburns down below his ears, which he probably thought impressed the ladies. I wondered if they ever did. The guy had the look of a loser, and it wasn't just because he was dead. He was flashy in a cheap, obvious way. His hair was greasy and looked as if he'd spent a lot of time combing it. Vainly, pretentiously. As if he could get a girl to meet him at a motel.

No, this was clearly the dude. Or most likely the dude. Or the Dude Most Likely, as in my abortive set of Man Most Likely jokes: "The man with the bullet in his head is most likely to be Mort." But that only works in French, and while I know the words for *man, head,* and *dead,* I don't know the word for *bullet.* Or *most likely,* for that matter. Le plus possible?

I was not thinking that while I stood looking at the body. I was hyperventilating and vacillating. Not from the shock of finding someone dead, which I have done now and then in the course of my checkered career. But from the dilemma in which I found myself.

The phone by the bed was the type with caller ID. I know because Alice has it. And it keeps a record of incoming calls. Alice had sometimes asked me to look one up, and I'd fumbled my way through the procedure enough times to realize I could fumble my way through it now.

Did I want to do that?

Or did I want to get the hell out of there?

Don't judge me too harshly. You gotta understand. I was out on bail. Which can be revoked, if you do anything to show you're not a good citizen. Like get arrested for murder. Getting arrested at this crime scene would probably be the end, if not of my life, of my liberty and pursuit of happiness. Richard, who had put up the bail bond, would not be pleased. Did he forfeit the money if I killed somebody else? See, I'd never been out on bail before. I'd been out on my own recognizance, but no one gives a damn if you forfeit that.

I'd certainly be going to jail. Which was kind of like Rome, where all roads led.

There were tissues on the night stand. I took one out, used it to push the button on the phone that activated caller ID history. The most recent number came up.

It wasn't mine.

Great.

Now, how did I exit the function?

I didn't remember.

Picking up the phone ought to do it.

I took another tissue, used it to lift the receiver, put it down.

Yes.

Everything reset.

My number wasn't in the caller ID, which meant I didn't have to be there to begin with, but I was, with a dead body, so what did I do now?

I was skipping down the stairs while I had that thought. Which kind of answered the question. I ran to the back of the house, slipped out through the unlocked kitchen door.

Yes, I polished the doorknob with the tissue.

I went around the house, not running, but not dawdling to take in the scenery either.

I hopped in my car and pulled out just as the police cars came down the street.

16

Richard Rosenberg looked annoyed. "Stanley. What the hell's going on? The girls have been fielding calls for you all afternoon."

"Really?"

"Didn't they tell you?"

"Wendy tried to say something on the way in, but I had to see you."

"I'll bet she did. She and Janet have been trying to beep you all day. Apparently, you turned off your beeper."

"I was busy. I didn't want to talk to any cops."

Richard's face darkened. "Why would the cops want to talk to you?"

"We have attorney-client privilege here?"

"We got more than that. We have twenty-five grand riding on you not fucking me over. So, tell me, what the hell stupid thing did you do now?"

I gave him the whole spiel. From MacAullif getting me the guy's credit card receipt to going in and finding him dead. I left out little things like being afraid I'd left my number on the caller ID. It wasn't on caller ID so it didn't matter. But aside from that I told him the whole schmear.

When I was done Richard sat there in helpless smoldering fury. I got the impression the only thing keeping him from turning me in was the fact it might cost him twenty-five thousand bucks.

"So," he said. "Does MacAullif know the guy whose address he gave you turned up dead?"

"Not as far as I know."

"I wouldn't think so. Otherwise there wouldn't be enough of you left to scrape off the floor." Richard snatched up the phone. "Any of those phone calls for Stanley from MacAullif? . . . Uh huh. Any of them official? . . . Yes, like cops . . . Uh huh." He hung up the phone. "Why would the police be looking for you?"

"I have no idea."

"Guess. Were you seen at the guy's house?"

"Not that I know of."

"Were you seen driving away?"

"Again, I don't think so."

"You didn't leave anything behind in the house that could be traced to you?"

My eyes flicked.

"Aha! Just what is it?"

"Ah, hell," I said, and told him the whole caller ID bit.

He was almost as scathing as Alice. Which wasn't fair. I was granting her the title without her having even competed. But there was no doubt that she would win.

Before Richard had another shot at the championship there came the sound of a ruckus in the outer office, the door slammed open, and MacAullif surged through. That was not supposed to happen. Richard had told the girls he was not to be disturbed. Not that I could fault them. There was no doubt they were doing their best. Wendy was actually clinging to the sergeant's leg. He shook her off, uttered a remark that probably would not have gotten him invited to be speaker at the local DAR. He grabbed me by the scruff of the neck, wheeled on Richard.

"Pardon the interruption, I need to borrow your employee."

"He's my client."

"I need to borrow your client. Don't worry, I'll return the unused portion."

He wrestled me toward the door.

"You can't do that," Richard said.

Apparently he could.

17

MacAullif dragged me out front, threw me in the back of his police car. He hopped in the front and took off.

"Where we going?"

"Shut up."

"Okay."

MacAullif had an unmarked car. I didn't know if the doors were locked, but if I wanted I could have hopped into the front seat, or reached up and strangled him, or put my hands over his eyes so he couldn't see what he was doing. If that occurred to MacAullif he didn't seem too concerned, just kept flying down the street.

"You mind telling me where we're going? It's not just an idle question. There are some places we probably shouldn't go."

"Like the Jersey Shore?"

A woman with a laundry cart leapt to safety, a look of sheer terror on her face.

"MacAullif!"

"I do you a favor. A favor I probably shouldn't do. A favor that is out of my jurisdiction. I pull a fast one, impersonate an officer — and don't say I *am* an officer, I mean a New Jersey officer. I pull it off and get you a name and address. And do you *investigate* the guy who lives at that address? No. You *kill* the guy who lives at that address."

"I didn't kill anyone."

"He's dead."

"That's not my fault."

"Oh, no? You *don't* investigate this guy, you think he's lying on some slab in the morgue, or out playing the ponies?"

"It doesn't have to be cause and effect."

"No, it doesn't *have* to be."

"It's probably not. Come on, MacAullif. The motel manager doesn't know you. The motel manager doesn't know you're connected to me. The motel manager doesn't know squat. The motel manager is just a guy giving you a name and address. Of someone we thought might be mixed up in the murder. Well, guess what? He *is*. This is *good* news. The death of the dipshit indicates we're on the right path."

"We're not on the right path. We're not on any path. We're on no path whatsofucking-ever, you and I. Is that clear?"

"What do you mean clear?"

MacAullif ran a red light and swerved around a bus, at the end of which he gave a perfunctory toot on the siren. "Don't be dense. I am not involved in this case. There is no *reason* to involve me in this case. If you *do* involve me in this case, I consider it a bad move and a breach of friendship. Is that clear?"

"Absolutely."

"So what are you gonna say when a cop asks you how you got this guy's address?"

"I'll tell him to go fuck himself."

MacAullif slammed on the brakes, pulled in next to a fire plug. He turned in his seat to grab me by the lapels long before the car stopped. "Asshole! I'm serious. Have you given any thought as to what you're going to say?"

"I want to call my lawyer."

"Don't pull that shit on me."

"No, that's what I'm gonna say. I'm gonna call my lawyer and I'm going to shut the fuck up. I've been arrested for murder and I'm out on bail."

I could feel some of the tension go out of MacAullif's body. "Well, that's something."

"Yeah, it's wonderful," I said. "It's not great news for *me,* but some of the people in this car ought to be happy."

"All right, let's have it. How bad is it?"

"I don't know. Why did you kick down Richard's door and drag me out of there?"

"You know why."

"Yeah, but the details matter. When you heard the guy was dead, how did you find out, and in what context? Was it brought to you personally, or was it just something you plucked out of the general pool of information?"

MacAullif exhaled noisily, shook his head. "If you were only half as good analyzing crime as you were at nitpicking my motivations. Okay, dipshit, you're closeted with your lawyer, you're not the least bit surprised to find the asshole's dead. Assuming you didn't kill him, what did you do?"

"Will you stay on that side of the seat?"

"Don't be a schmuck."

I gave MacAullif a rundown of the situation. I can't say I improved his mood any.

"So, the cops haven't picked you up yet," he mused.

"I like to think of it as they haven't picked me up."

"Fat chance. Suspect out on bail when a second murder occurs. I think even *you* would want to talk to him."

"I'm not so sure."

"Why?"

"How do I know the two crimes are even related? The cops don't know that."

"Of course they know that."

"But they don't credit it. They're not buying the guy-next-door theory. There's no reason for them to even notice."

"Now you're dreaming."

"They don't credit the guy next door because they think I did it. If the guy next door is connected, I'm no longer a suspect."

"Dream on."

"Come on, MacAullif, they can't have it both ways."

"Oh, no? Try this. You're connected. The guy next door's connected. You're both connected. When you get picked up, you try to put the blame on him. He doesn't take kindly to this, and the end result is you have to rub him out."

"Jesus Christ. How'd you put that together so fast?"

"I'm a cop. It's what I do."

"Interpret extraneous facts to frame an innocent man?"

"Well, it's more challenging. The guilty ones have the disadvantage of having actually done it."

"It's good to hear you say that."

"Why?"

"It means you're getting your sense of

humor back."

"Oh, you think so? Just wait until that dumb fucking motel manager IDs me as the guy who got the address. Then we'll see how much sense of humor I have about this."

"I'd kind of like to head that off."

"Oh?"

"I was thinking if we could solve this thing —"

MacAullif exploded. "Jesus Christ! You never learn, do you? You bring me a steaming pile of shit and expect me to find a pony. Well, I ain't playing."

"You object to catching this killer?"

"I got no problem catching this killer. As far as the Jersey cops are concerned, I just caught him. I could drive you there now, collect the reward."

"Except they'd want to know how I got the line on my victim."

"You're pushing your luck."

"Come on, MacAullif. What you said before. About me and the guy next door working to set this guy up. That didn't happen, but something similar did. You and I have the inside track in knowing that. Now, setting aside the great solution that I killed this guy, how does he wind up dead?"

"Which guy?"

"The second guy. The mafia guy. Vinnie

93

what's-his-face."

"He winds up dead so he won't talk."

"What's he gonna say?"

"He's gonna say he rented the motel room for high-level wise guy whatever-the-hell-his-name-is. Who, as far as he knows, was shackin' up with a broad. It would have come as a real shock to him to find out the guy in the motel room next to the one he rented wound up dead."

"If that's true, why is he dangerous?"

"He's dangerous because he can name the guy who rented the room. He doesn't know that makes him dangerous, but it does. Someone else knows it makes him dangerous."

"Yeah, the guy who killed him."

"No," MacAullif said. "The guy who *tipped off* the guy who killed him. The way I see it, there's only one person that could be."

"The motel manager?"

"That's how I figure."

"You're right. We gotta take him apart and see what makes him tick."

"No, we don't!"

"Why not?"

"We'd just give him reason to go to the cops."

"Not if he's the guy who tipped off the
94

killer. If he's in on this thing, he's not running to the cops."

"Assuming he tipped off the killer," MacAullif said. "Which is still just an assumption."

"Who else could have done it?"

"I don't know. But my ass is hanging fairly far out on this one. And prodding the motel manager could fuck me good. Which is why you're not going to do that."

"Oh."

"Oh? What do you mean, 'oh'? Are you telling me you already did?"

"Of course not."

"Good. Because talking to the motel manager would be just about the stupidest thing you could do right now. Short of talking to the dead guy's wife."

I blinked.

MacAullif nearly gagged. "Oh, my God!"

"MacAullif —"

"I don't believe it! Are you telling me after you found the dead mobster's body you spoke to the widow?"

"No, of course not."

"Did you talk to her before?"

"Well —"

"You did, didn't you?" MacAullif's voice was rising. "You talked to her *before* you found the mobster's body, but *after* I got

95

the credit card receipt from the motel manager. You talked to her to see if she'd hire you! To investigate the murder of her husband! Whom she suspects you of killing! You figured if you were going to check out the guy anyway, you might as well have someone pay for it!"

"It wasn't the money."

"No, of *course* not," MacAullif said scathingly. "That would be *logical.* That would make *sense.* That would be a simple, basic motive anyone could relate to. But you — correct me if I'm wrong — you want her to hire you because you want to convince her you're a basically good person who would never harm her husband."

"I'm accused of murder. She's a witness against me."

"Exactly! She's the last person in the world you should be talking to! But you figure you can charm her! What did you do, appeal to her better nature? Show her your dick?"

MacAullif wrenched the car out of the spot, sped down the street.

"Where we going?"

MacAullif said nothing, just kept heading west.

"My car's back there."

"I know where your car is."

He got on the West Side Highway, headed uptown.

"It's nice of you to drive me home, MacAullif, but I'd rather have my car."

We seemed to be passing a lot of cars. I peeked at the dashboard. MacAullif was doing ninety.

"I guess if you're a cop you got a right to drive any speed you want."

MacAullif ignored me. If anything, he accelerated.

"That's my exit," I said as we passed Ninety-sixth Street.

MacAullif zigzagged through traffic, went up the ramp to the Cross Bronx Expressway and the George Washington Bridge. He kept right, swerved around the entrance to Martha Washington, the bridge's lower level.

"We going to Jersey?" I said. I remembered Al Pacino saying the same thing in *The Godfather* when Michael Corleone was in the car with Sollozzo, and his heart was in his throat because they were heading for Jersey, and the restaurant where they'd planted the gun in the bathroom for him was in the Bronx. "I thought you said it would be a bad idea to talk to the motel manager."

MacAullif pulled out in front of an eighteen-wheeler, passed a slow-moving panel truck and got in the right-hand lane to exit.

We weren't going to the motel. I had a sudden paranoid thought, *Good god, he is going to turn me in to the cops.* Which shows how stressed out I was. Because that couldn't possibly compute. After all, what conceivable explanation could he come up with for putting me under arrest?

We weren't going to the police station either. MacAullif got on the Palisades Parkway, heading north, and hit the gas.

One good thing, he was obeying the speed limit. At least compared to New York. He was only doing seventy. I guess because he wasn't a Jersey cop and couldn't count on their cooperation. Not because he was afraid they'd stop him and take charge of his prisoner.

"Where the hell are we going?"

MacAullif steamed on by exit one and kept going north. Finally he slowed, put on his blinker.

I looked.

There was a roadside rest area up ahead on the right. Not with amenities. Just a place you could pull off the road and park.

MacAullif drove in. There was no one around. He parked behind a grove of trees, killed the motor.

"Get out."

My mouth fell open. I wasn't Michael Corleone in *The Godfather.* I was Adriana in *The Sopranos,* Chris's cop-collaborating girlfriend being taken for a ride by Bruce Springsteen's guitarist, Silvio.

"Am I getting whacked?"

"I wish."

He jerked his thumb.

I opened the door, got out, waited for MacAullif to join me.

He didn't.

Before it dawned on me what he was doing, MacAullif started the car and drove off.

18

"I can't believe he left you there," Alice said.

It was not the first time she had said so. I guess her disbelief was ongoing. I had accepted the situation. At least the fact that it happened. Of course, I had a lot longer to think about it, having had to get home from Jersey.

It involved crossing the northbound lanes of the Palisades Parkway, not fun in rush hour, to get to the southbound lanes. Then crossing the southbound lanes, slightly easier, to get to the right-hand side of the road.

Then trying to hitchhike on the Palisades Parkway, a fruitless, bad, and illegal enterprise. At least no one tried to pick me up, which probably would have resulted in a ten-car pileup or me getting arrested or both.

Then it required walking several miles south to exit one, I couldn't tell you how many as my internal odometer is somewhat faulty. Then attempting to hitchhike south on 9W for several blocks, until finally giving up and just walking the damn thing.

Then taking a bus over the George Washington Bridge, catching a subway downtown to pick up my car, and then driving home.

If you're wondering, yes, I had my cell phone, yes, I could have called Alice to come get me, but that would have required her going downtown to get my car and fighting her way through rush-hour traffic to pick me up, with the end result that *she* would have had all that time to come to grips with MacAullif stranding me in New Jersey, and move on to new subject matter, such as what I had done to deserve it.

Not that she didn't get there anyway.

"So, MacAullif is pissed off because you found another body and happened to run away without telling the cops?"

"What's your point?"

"What the hell were you thinking? You're out on bail for a murder so you go breaking into a mobster's house."

"I thought my number was on his caller ID."

"Yes, you did. Tell me, what would have been easier to explain, getting caught in the guy's house, or having dialed him on your cell phone, a call that could have been made from anywhere on earth?"

"There's still some pockets you can't get service."

"It's not funny, Stanley. This whole thing's got me freaked out."

"I didn't do anything."

"Yes, I know. But I'm not going to be on your jury."

"This isn't going to court."

"You copping a plea?"

"I thought it wasn't funny."

"It isn't. I'm trying to boost my spirits by ridiculing you."

"How's that working?"

"It's not really satisfying." Alice shook her head. "I can't believe you ran away."

"I didn't run away."

"You didn't stay. You found a dead body and you took off."

"I had to."

"Why?"

"If the cops found me there, they'd think I did it."

"With what gun?"

"How the hell should I know what gun?"

"You can't shoot a guy without a gun. Was there a gun there?"

"Not that I noticed. There could have been one under the body. There could have been one under the bed. There could have been one in the trash. There could have been one anywhere in the house. It didn't matter where. If there was one there at all, the cops would assume I used it and that would be that. Even if there wasn't a gun, there was no way I could explain what I was doing there."

"You were investigating the murder."

"How did I get a line on the guy? If I don't tell them, they suspect me of murder. If I do tell them, I implicate MacAullif."

"MacAullif left you on the Palisades Parkway."

"Right. I should pay him back by getting him convicted of a felony?"

"That's silly."

"Conspiring to conceal a crime is a felony."

"You didn't conspire to conceal a crime. You conspired to *solve* a crime. It's not the same thing."

"Tell it to the cops."

"Stanley. Wake up. You didn't kill anyone. You didn't *commit* a crime. You can't conspire to conceal a crime that isn't a crime."

"You don't have to sell me, Alice."

"It sounds like I do. If you want to feel guilty about getting MacAullif in trouble, you gotta remember that is provisional on you being convicted of murder. Do I have to explain to you what torturous logic is in play here?"

"No. You have to explain it to MacAullif. Because he's the one making the claim."

"Oh, give me a break. MacAullif may rant and rave and curse you to the high heavens, but even he doesn't think you're going to get convicted of murder and he's going to be charged as an accessory and kicked off the force. Not in his wildest dreams."

"I don't have to get convicted to get him in trouble. If it turns out he's been meddling in the case his ass is grass no matter what the outcome."

"Great. Just great. And who is this schmuck who got killed?"

"The guy who rented the room next to the other schmuck who got killed."

"Which could be totally unrelated."

"Not any more, or he wouldn't be dead. Which is why MacAullif getting a line on him while he was still alive is such a red flag."

"Are you sure he was still alive?"

"What do you mean?"

"Is it possible he was killed *before* MacAullif found out who he was?"

"We don't know the time of death. And

the way things stand, nobody's about to tell me."

"Would it be a lot better if the guy was dead when MacAullif was asking?"

"No."

"Why not? If he was dead, MacAullif couldn't have given you the guy's address so you could kill him."

"If he was dead, everyone's gonna think MacAullif *knew* he was dead and that's why he was asking."

"If MacAullif knew he was dead, why would he have to ask?"

"Huh?"

"How could MacAullif know he was dead and not know who he is? I mean, 'Someone's dead, I wonder who. Let me ask the motel manager.' " Alice shrugged her shoulders, spread her hands. "See? It doesn't compute."

"No. 'The *guy who rented the motel room* is dead, let me find out who he is.' "

"MacAullif knows the guy rented the motel room but doesn't know who he is?"

"That's right."

"Then how does he know he rented the motel room? 'The guy who rented the motel room is dead. I wonder who he is. Let's ask the motel manager.' "

"Stop, stop, stop." It was like being stung

by a hive of bees. "Alice, all your points are valid. You don't have to convince me, you have to convince a very skeptical New Jersey cop, who isn't gonna care that all your points are valid. All he's gonna care is, someone's dead, and someone's messing with the evidence. In his humble opinion, which may be supported by very faulty logic."

"Can't you just point out what I did?"

"No."

"Why not?"

"I'm not as good at arguing and I don't have nice tits."

"Stanley."

"I'm serious. All the arguments in the world aren't going to help. The only thing that's going to persuade this cop is finding out who did it."

"And MacAullif won't investigate?"

"That's an understatement."

"And he doesn't want you to investigate for yourself?"

"No."

"And you feel you have to do what he wants because you got him into trouble."

"In a way."

"What way would that be?"

"All, right, that's how I feel."

"So you can't investigate?"

"Yeah."

"So who can?"

19

Mike Sallingsworth looked older than the last time I'd seen him. Which was strange, since I looked exactly the same. I'd hired Mike once, way back when. Now I was looking to hire him again.

Sallingsworth was a private investigator from Atlantic City. It occurred to me that I only hired private eyes when I was in New Jersey. Mike sat at the kitchen table, sipped his scotch, ran his fingers through his rapidly thinning hair.

"I'm retired," he said.

"For the night?"

"Don't be a jerk," Mike said. It was two in the afternoon. "I retired three years ago. Got tired of the routine. I got a little bit saved up, enough to spend the winters in Florida."

"What do you do for excitement?"

"Not work. You can't believe how stimulating that is. Get up, walk out, take the air.

Come back when I damn well feel like it. There is a simple joy in not working that is an activity in itself."

"How'd you like a job?"

"I would not like a job. I like this scotch. You always did bring me good scotch. On the other hand, you always brought me uninspiring work."

"It may not have inspired you. It happened to clear up a murder or two."

"As I recall, I never had to lift a finger."

"That's because you're a wealth of information. I'm wondering if that's still true. What do you know about the Jersey Shore?"

"I know enough to stay away from it."

"Why is that?"

"There are two kinds of people on the Jersey Shore. Those that are connected, and those that are not connected. Those that are connected are dangerous. Those that are not connected are dangerous."

"Why is that?"

"Because you can't always tell which is which." Sallingsworth poured another scotch, sloshed it around in his glass. "Can I assume you are talking about people who are connected?"

"That would be a safe assumption."

"Safe for you. Dangerous for me. Luckily, I'm retired."

"Just because you're retired doesn't mean you don't know things."

"Just because I'm retired doesn't mean I don't like living."

"I assure you, you won't be quoted."

"Can you assure me you weren't followed here?"

"Why would anyone follow me?"

"Gee, I don't know. Would it have anything to do with your being arrested for murder?"

"You know about that?"

"Was it supposed to be a secret?"

"No, but this is Atlantic City. We're talking the Ft. Lee, Englewood Cliffs, Teaneck area."

"Murder's murder. And it's not every day the perp gets caught at the scene."

"I didn't do it."

"Clever defense. How's it working for you?"

"Not so good. The point is the guy who got killed isn't in the mob. He worked for Aflac in New York."

"Really? With the duck?"

"Yeah, the duck. If you heard about that you probably heard about Vinnie Carbone. Got whacked yesterday afternoon."

"So I understand. Only in that case they got no suspect."

"No, they don't. I'm wondering if that's

because the cops tread lightly when the mob's involved."

"Heaven forbid."

"With regard to Vinnie Carbone's mob connection. You wouldn't happen to know what that was?"

Sallingsworth sighed, pushed back the bottle. "Oh, dear. Just when things were going so well. Let me lay it out for you. You lead the cops to me. I give you the name of someone in the mob. You lead the cops to him. The mobster doesn't like cops being led to him, so he inquires how this might have happened. He traces it back to me, and my retirement comes to a sudden and rather unpleasant conclusion."

"That sounds like a worst-case scenario."

"Well, it's certainly not the best. So, could you think of any reason under the sun why I should help you?"

"Absolutely."

"Do tell."

"Your theory is if you tell me how to find this mobster and I lead the cops to him, he'll be able to trace it back to me and therefore to you. Now assume you don't tell me how to find him. I'm going to find him and lead the cops to him anyway. Then when he starts tracing things back, he's going to find I called on you. He won't know

111

if you told me anything or not, he'll just whack you for practice."

Mike poured another drink. "Not going to happen. And I'll tell you why. If you get a lead on the mobster, it will be from someone else. And when he starts looking for the guy who ratted him out, he'll find that guy, not me."

"Okay. Try this. If you tell me, I'll go away and you'll never see me again. If you don't tell me, I'll keep coming back and asking until you tell me or you're dead."

"You'd do that?"

"Of course not. On the other hand, I don't really wanna take the fall for murder. All right, look. You don't wanna give me a lead to the mob, give me a lead to someone who can give me a lead to the mob."

"It's the same thing."

"Not really. It's one more degree of separation. It's the same thing you just said about finding the other guy first. Plus I won't give your name to the guy you give me, which breaks the chain."

Sallingsworth studied my face. "You must be really desperate. What the hell's going on?"

I gave Sallingsworth a rundown of what happened. When I was done he shook his head.

"I don't know how you ever lasted this long."

"I didn't retire."

"That's where you made your big mistake."

"Can you help me?"

"Nothing's gonna help you. Your best shot is go home, watch TV, pretend this never happened."

"You forget I have this court date for murder."

"Your attorney any good? Your best shot is beating the rap. Trying to solve the crime will probably get you killed."

"Thanks for the encouragement."

"My pleasure."

"You can't help me at all?"

Sallingsworth shook his head. "Wouldn't be prudent."

I sighed, got up. "Well, enjoy your retirement, in case I don't see you again."

Sallingsworth nodded, raised his glass. "Thanks for the scotch."

20

As if I didn't have enough problems, now I had to investigate a homicide without getting an elderly detective from Atlantic City whacked. It was just the sort of moral dilemma I needed to complete my already impossible situation.

I drove back from Atlantic City feeling mildly irritated that my old friend, Mike Sallingsworth, didn't really want to die. So who could I ask for advice now? Not Richard. Not MacAullif. Not Alice. All had weighed in with the universally accepted position that I had totally fucked up. I had come to see Sallingsworth because I needed to get a line on the dead man without involving MacAullif. Now I had to get a line on the guy without involving Sallingsworth.

As I came up on the Elizabeth exit I wondered if the cops were done with his house. The thought intrigued me. Would there be a crime scene ribbon across the door?

Could it hurt to just drive by?

I could think of many ways it could hurt to just drive by, starting with MacAullif twisting my head off my shoulders and ending with New Jersey cops gleefully waterboarding me. Neither seemed a desirable outcome, nor did either seem likely. The cops would have no reason to watch the house. It would not occur to them there might be something in it of some value to the killer. Or the man most likely to be cast in the role.

As I got off the New Jersey Turnpike and drove toward the place, it occurred to me I was risking getting indicted for a second count of murder and all I was concerned with was whether I got a couple of other guys in trouble. I figured that made me one hell of a good guy.

Or stupid as shit.

There was a crime scene ribbon over Vinnie's front door. Aside from that, there was no indication that there had been a crime. There was certainly no police presence, at least that I could see.

Not that it mattered.

I wasn't going in, was I?

The front door opened and a young

woman came out. An absolute knockout in a cheap and flashy way. That was prejudiced on my part, predicated no doubt on Vinnie's Jersey Shore connection, but there's cheap and flashy and there's cheap and flashy. The girl had big boobs, featured in skin-tight spandex in a manner that seemed to imply she spent some money getting big boobs just so she could flaunt them in this fashion. Her blond hair looked like it came out of a bottle. She wore false eyelashes, thick eyeliner, and too much eye shadow. Her bright red lipstick was the only eye-catcher between the eyes and the boobs.

She slipped under the crime scene ribbon, looked in both directions, and came down the front path. If she hadn't glanced around furtively I might have seen the manila envelope in her hand for what it was, a manila envelope, and not for something she had just pilfered from the crime scene.

She hopped into a red Prius and took off.

I followed at a discreet distance. At least that's what I keep reading in detective stories. Actually, I'm not quite sure what a discreet distance is. I think it's one where you don't get spotted on the one hand, or lose the person on the other.

I followed her about fifteen miles south to a beauty parlor in a strip mall. I wondered if she was getting a haircut. It occurred to me she could use it. I chided myself for the thought. I was trying not to stereotype the woman, but it was hard.

It was harder when it turned out she was a hairdresser. I mean she not only looked like that, her job was making other people look like that.

Perhaps I was misjudging her. The first woman she worked on didn't have teased hair at all. She had a wavy shag sort of thing, and from what I could see the Jersey Girl was giving it a perfectly conservative trim.

Watching the woman cut hair was not exactly the optimal outcome I'd hoped for when I'd seen her coming out of the dead guy's house. I wondered if I should get a haircut. That seemed a poor option. There were four women working, so I'd have to do some pretty nimble-footed maneuvering to make sure I got her. And I wasn't sure they cut men's hair. There wasn't a guy in the place. Breaking the gender barrier didn't seem the best way of being inconspicuous.

I thought of calling Alice and asking if she needed a haircut. I can't begin to tell you all the reasons why that seemed like a poor idea. It occurred to me if I were a real detective I would have a female operative I'd call in for just these occasions. Of course, if I were a real detective I probably wouldn't blunder into such awful scrapes.

I thought of my old buddy, Fred Lazar, the guy who actually got me into the game. He'd have had a female operative, only he, like Sallingsworth, was retired.

I'd have retired too, if I didn't need the money. Not that I minded working, but being a fall guy was wearing me down.

So what could I do now?

Watching the Jersey Girl as she wielded her scissors, there was one thing that occurred to me.

When she went through the beauty parlor door there was nothing in her hands.

The Prius was parked out of sight from the beauty parlor window. At least out of sight from chair number three, which was where Jersey Girl was working. The hairdresser in the chair closest to the window could see it, but then it wasn't her car.

I strolled down the street, walked casually by the Prius. Wondered how to get in.

A clothes hanger down the crack between the top of the window and the doorframe used to be an option, back in the days when door locks were round and had a little heads on them you could get under and pry up. Jersey Girl's door locks were shiny as a baby's bottom with nary a lip of any kind. So Car Thief Trick number 101 was out.

A police slim jim might have worked, since that didn't grab the knob but slid right into the mechanism of the lock. Only I didn't have a slim jim on account of not happening to be on the police force.

I wondered if MacAullif had one.

I wasn't standing there thinking all this, by the way, I had continued on up the street. It was taking me away from my objective, but I needed a plausible reason to turn around.

No, you don't, I told myself. If I wasn't being followed, no one could possibly give a damn. If I was being followed, they were already on to me, so what if they saw me change direction?

I turned around, walked back to the car, tried the passenger side door.

It opened.

No coat hangers, slim jims, car thieves, or police officers involved.

I slid into the passenger seat, popped the glove compartment. It was the first place I looked, largely because it was right in front of me. I found an owner's manual, still in plastic, most likely unread, and a mountain of receipts. I wondered if knowing what this young woman had bought could possibly help me.

I slammed the glove compartment, turned around, looked in the back seat.

There was a lightweight overcoat wadded up in the corner, and that was it. I shook it out, patted the pockets, found nothing, checked for an inner pocket which the coat didn't have. I wadded it up, threw it back in the corner.

On the floor on the far side of the driver's seat was the trunk release. I wondered if I should pop the trunk. Jersey Girl hadn't, so there wasn't much point. But I didn't have anything else. I leaned over, popped the trunk.

I got out, walked around the car. Tried to appear like a casual motorist as opposed to a car thief. I'm not quite sure of the distinction, but I gave it my best shot.

I raised the lid of the trunk.

Jackpot!

Right there in plain sight was a woman's leather purse, big enough to have held the manila envelope. I picked it up nonchalantly, as if performing a task for my wife, retrieving something she had sent me back to the car to get.

I pulled the purse open wide.

No manila envelopes sprang to view. But I couldn't really see. I stuck my hand in the purse, was instantly disappointed. I could tell from how far my hand went in without encountering anything that, unless she had folded the envelope up, it was not there. Of course, all of that was dismissing the reality that since I hadn't seen her open the trunk and put the envelope in the purse, there was no way it could be.

On the other hand, unless she stuffed it in her pants on her way into the beauty parlor, it had to be somewhere.

I fumbled deeper in the purse.

My hand hit something cold and hard.

I pulled it out.

It was a gun.

I immediately leaned further over the trunk, shielding my find from prying eyes with my body, as if I were a nervous husband not wanting people to see I was looking in my wife's purse.

All right, all right, that wasn't my intention. The appearance of the gun had short-circuited my nervous system, rendering my dissembling and play-acting moot, and left me simply reacting on the basic instinct of not wanting anyone to see what I had found.

I angled my body between the car and the sidewalk and inspected the weapon.

It was a revolver. A Smith & Wesson revolver. A .38-caliber Smith & Wesson revolver, but that's a guess. I've seen MacAullif's gun, not his police issue, his private gun, and that's a thirty-eight. I'd handled it once, empty.

This gun was not empty.

This gun had bullets.

I popped the cylinder, dumped them out. In more time than it takes to tell it. I handled the gun gingerly trying not to shoot myself in the foot.

There were five bullets and one empty shell casing.

I sniffed the barrel.

The gun had been recently fired. How recently, I couldn't tell you, but there was the unmistakable smell of gunpowder. I'd have to do some research to find out how long the smell would last.

I jammed the bullets back in the cylinder, replaced the empty shell, and stuck the gun back in the purse. I knew I shouldn't be doing it. I was leaving fingerprints all over the place. But there was no help for it. I couldn't take out a handkerchief and start polishing bullets in the middle of the street.

I put the purse back in the trunk, slammed it shut.

The discovery of the gun had distracted me from my initial objective. I still had no idea what had happened to the manila envelope.

I got back in the car again. Felt under the passenger's seat. There was nothing there. I tried the driver's seat. There was nothing there either.

I got out of the car, opened the back door, searched under the seats from behind. There was nothing under the passenger's seat. I tried the driver's seat.

My hand hit something.

I reached down, tugged it out.

It was the manila envelope.

It was clasped. I unclasped it, reached in, pulled out an eight-by-ten glossy, color photograph of Jersey Girl.

She was naked.

She was sitting on the bed with her knees bent and her legs wide open. She was looking straight at the camera with a wicked, teasing, come-hither smile.

I put the photo back in the envelope, clasped it, slid the envelope back under the seat.

I got out, walked back to my car, whipped out my cell phone and called home.

"Yeah?" Alice said. "What's up?"

"I won't be home for dinner."

21

She got off work at eight.

I wondered where she'd go. Her boyfriend was dead. It occurred to me she might have more than one. I mean, if she could go back to work the day after he was killed, maybe he wasn't that big a deal in her life, any rather revealing photos notwithstanding.

I'd been staking out the beauty parlor from across the street and not feeling all that happy about it. I'd staked out the motel and someone wound up dead. I'd staked out the wise guy's house and someone wound up dead. Not that I was getting a complex or anything, still I was mighty happy when the woman walked out alive. Of course the evening was yet young.

Jersey Girl hopped in the Prius and drove out of town. I had no idea where she was going or what I was going to do. All I knew was I was following a hot babe with a gun. If she took the leather purse out of the trunk

I was going to be on high alert.

As we drove out of town the houses were bigger and farther apart. She turned in the driveway of one that was very nice indeed. It looked like more than a hairdresser could afford.

It was. Jersey Girl didn't live in the big house. She had an apartment over the garage. That was too bad. I was hoping I could just look up her address. But, no, she wasn't the one who lived there. Of course she would have the same mail address, unless she had a post office box, which was probably a good bet. There was only one mailbox out by the road, and the hoity-toity owners of the big house wouldn't want her stuff mixed in with their mail. I was unfairly maligning them, but nothing in this case seemed fair, at least not to me.

She got out of her car, opened the rear door, reached under the seat and pulled out the manila envelope. She closed the door, popped the trunk and retrieved the leather purse. She zapped the car locked and went up the wooden steps.

So, I was dealing with the type of ditz who locks it in the driveway with the trunk empty and leaves it unlocked on the street with beaver shots and a loaded gun.

Jersey Girl went up the steps, unlocked

the door to her apartment over the garage, and went in.

Okay, what did I do now? Stake out the garage. At least it only had one exit.

The minute I thought that, I immediately began to doubt it. What if that's not the only entrance? What if there's an interior stair-case leading down into the garage? So she goes up the stairs, into the apartment, down into the garage, through the breezeway, and even now she's romping around in the great big house.

But why in the world would she do that?

Unfortunately, I had an answer. Because she spotted me following her and she's play-ing a game.

Nonsense. She's a hairdresser and she's alert enough to spot a tail?

Well, she did have a loaded gun in her car. People with loaded guns tended to be wary. Particularly people with loaded guns which had been recently fired and whose boy-friends had been recently shot.

Bullshit. She lives over the garage and she hasn't got a clue.

I got out of my car, slammed the door, crossed the street. I figured I'd better do it before I thought about it. Because if I thought about it I wouldn't, and I clearly had to do something. I went up the wooden steps and banged on the door.

She opened it a crack and peered out. "Yes?"

I flipped open my leather folder with my ID. "Detective Hastings. Sorry to bother you. Just a few questions."

"But I already told you everything I know."

"Sorry, ma'am, just routine, I won't be long."

"I'm making dinner."

"I won't stop you. Just doing my job."

She sighed, opened the door, let me in.

Jersey Girl had changed out of her working gear and slipped on a baby blue kimono. It was tied at her waist with a sash, but it was rather loose and tended to gape. I got the impression she had taken off her bra. In light of the picture I had just seen, the effect was disturbing. I felt an electric tingle through my body in general and some areas in particular.

She padded ahead of me into the room.

Jersey Girl lived in a modest studio apartment. It had a double bed against the far wall, a small couch and coffee table, and a kitchen nook in the corner. If she was really making dinner, she was just getting started, because there was nothing on the kitchen counter.

She led me to the kitchen table instead of the couch. I got the hint. If I were asking her questions I could damn well get it over with and not make myself comfortable. She sat at kitchen table. I opted to stand, not entirely so I could see down the kimono.

"When was the last time you saw Vinnie alive?"

"You asked me this already."

"I didn't ask you anything," I corrected. "I can't go on someone else's report. They could be wrong. I need it firsthand. When was the last time you saw him alive?"

"The day before yesterday."

"How come?"

"What do you mean, how come? We weren't living together. I wanted to move in, but he wouldn't let me."

"Why not?"

"I don't know. I think he wanted to be free to play around."

"You don't seem too broken up."

She looked up angrily. "What's the matter? You want me in tears? I'm sure if you work hard at it you can make me cry. Is that what you really want to do?"

"Not at all. I just want some answers to some questions."

"What do you want to know?"

"Do you own a gun?"

"Of course not. Why would I own a gun?"

"You tell me."

"I told you. I don't own a gun."

"You ever carry one?"

"What do you mean?"

"You may not own one, but did you ever use one? You ever carry one around?"

"Only target shooting. Vinnie used to teach me."

"Vinnie had a gun?"

"Yeah."

"Ever loan it to you?"

"What are you getting at?"

"Vinnie was shot. So far we haven't found the gun that did it. So we're interested in any gun he was connected with."

"You think he was shot with his own gun?"

"We don't know what gun he was shot with. We're investigating all possibilities."

"Yeah, well that's not possible. Try something else."

"You don't have a gun on you?"

"No."

"Vinnie never loaned you his gun and forgot to take it back?"

"Of course not. Why would he do that?"

"I don't know why. I'm asking if he did."

"I tell you, no."

"I can't search this place without a search warrant. But let me ask you something. Is there anything here you don't want me to see?"

"Of course not."

"Then do you mind if I take a look?"

"Of course I mind. I don't want you going through my things."

"But you don't have anything you don't want me to see. For instance, the roaches in the ashtray on the coffee table. You wouldn't want me to look at that and come to the conclusion you've been smoking pot."

Her face fell. "Oh, come on."

"It's a good thing I didn't see them. You know why I didn't see them? I didn't see them because I'm not looking for them. I'm not looking for anything but a gun. Anything I find that isn't a gun I don't give a tinker's damn about. You know what that means?"

She frowned. "No."

"Neither do I, but it's something people always say."

She crinkled up her nose. "You're weird."

"No, I'm single minded. I want to find out who killed Vinnie. I'm betting you do too."

"Of course I do."

"So help me out. Let me look around, convince myself you don't have a gun. I'm not interested in your intimate apparel, sex toys, or recreational drugs. Am I making myself clear?"

"Now, see here."

"All I care about is do you have a gun."

"No."

"Prove it."

The leather purse was on a chair by the door. "Your bag over there. That looks big enough to hold a gun. If I were going to carry a gun, that's where I would keep it. Is there a gun in that bag?"

"No."

"Would you mind showing me?"

"Why?"

"Because I'm asking nice. If it's nothing, I'll leave you alone. If it's something, I'll have a few questions."

She gave me a look, flounced over and picked up the purse. On her way back to the table she frowned.

"What's the matter?"

"It's heavier than I thought."

"Is that so?"

"No, that's *not* so, Mr. Smarty Pants. It may surprise you to know a woman happens to have a lot of other things in her purse."

"I'm glad to hear it. What you got?"

She plunked the bag down on the kitchen table. "Here, I'll show you. I got keys. And

a compact. And a lipstick."
She pulled out the gun.

22

It was one of those good-news, bad-news situations. I wanted to catch her with a gun. I didn't want *her* to catch *me* with a gun. I had to act fast before she trained it on me. I reached out quickly, twisted it from her grasp.

"Let's not point that at anyone, shall we?"

Her eyes were wide. "I don't know where that came from. I didn't know it was there."

She was so fixated on the gun she failed to notice her kimono had fallen open and her left nipple was sticking out. I noticed, which is a sad commentary on the state of the married man. Even with a loaded gun in play, my attention could be distracted.

I held up the gun. "This isn't yours?"

"No."

"You didn't know it was in your purse?"

"No. I have no idea how it got there."

"Is it Vinnie's?"

"How should I know?"

133

I wasn't staring, but something drew her attention to the open kimono. She pulled it closed, said, "I don't like this. You come in here, accuse me of having a gun, look in one place and it's there. How do I know you didn't plant that on your way in?"

"You met me at the door. You weren't carrying a purse. I didn't go near that chair. Is it Vinnie's?"

"I tell you, I don't know."

"Does it look like Vinnie's?"

"I don't know."

"Yes, you do. You fired it. Take a look. Is there anything about it that's different than Vinnie's?"

"I don't know."

"You haven't looked."

She set her jaw, looked at the gun. "I can't tell. I'd have to have it in my hand."

"I'd rather have it in mine."

"You don't trust me?"

"Small problem there. You told me you didn't have a gun."

"I don't have a gun. That's not my gun."

"Uh huh." I sniffed the barrel. "It's been fired recently. You wouldn't know anything about that?"

"I don't know anything about any gun. My god, you're worse than the other guy."

"What other guy?"

134

"The other cop. In here, asking questions."

"But he didn't find a gun?"

"He didn't look."

"Too bad."

"No, it isn't. I didn't have a gun. You planted it on me. I don't know how you did it, but you did."

I dumped out the bullets, showed her the empty shell. "There's been one shot fired."

"That's impossible."

"How is it impossible? It's not your gun."

Her eyes shifted.

"See, you can't get away with it. You kept the purse locked in the trunk of your car. Why would you do that if you didn't know about the gun?"

"Who says I did?"

"I say you did. I was waiting for you to come home. You drove up, popped the trunk, took out the purse. Now, you wanna play games, it's up to you. You can answer questions here or down at the station."

"Aw, gee."

She looked on the verge of tears. I wondered if that was just an act. If so, I wondered if she'd "accidently" let the kimono fall open again.

"So, let's try it again. Where did you get the gun?"

"I . . ."

"Yes?"

She exhaled noisily. The kimono rustled. "It's like you said. It's Vinnie's gun. He loaned it to me. Forgot to take it back."

"And you've been carrying it ever since?"

"No. I haven't been carrying it. I just had it. After he got killed I got scared, so I put it in my purse."

"You thought someone might be after you?"

"Yeah."

"Isn't that a little melodramatic?"

"Vinnie's dead."

"What's that got to do with you?"

"I don't know what it's got to do with me. I don't know what it's got to do with him. Someone shot him in his house. I've been in that house. I could have been there then. It could be me on the floor."

During that outburst her kimono had loosened perceptively. She didn't seem to be wearing any panties either. Visions of Sharon Stone in *Basic Instinct* danced in my head.

"So you put the gun in your purse?"

"Yeah."

"Where was it?"

"What?"

"Where was it before you put it in your purse?"

"Oh."

"Hadn't thought of that?"

"Didn't realize it was important," she snapped. "It was in my dresser drawer."

"Had it been fired?"

"I didn't think so. But it must have."

"How did that happen?"

"I don't know. I guess I didn't reload after target practice. It's been a long time. I don't remember."

"The gun has never been out of the house from the last time you took target practice until you put it in your car?"

"That's right. So it can't have anything to do with the murder. It's unimportant, see?"

She cinched the kimono around her, struck a haughty pose. She must have thought she was winning.

"So if we test fire this gun and put the bullet on a comparison microscope with the fatal bullet they won't match?"

"Of course not."

"I hope you're right. Technically, I should take you in. The gun is evidence, needs to be checked out."

"You don't need me. Take the gun. What do you need me for?"

"You had the gun in your possession. That

137

makes you a person of interest."

She leaned in. "Ah, come on. Give me a break."

"Did the cop who talked to you take you in?"

"No, he just talked to me here. It's where I live. It's where you'll always find me. What can I do to show you I'm on the level?"

That was as close to a proposition as I'd gotten from a near-naked woman in some time. Not that I was about to act on it. Or would have, even without a murder charge hanging over my head. But I had a small problem. With the appearance of the gun, there was no way I could avoid taking her in. And I wasn't a cop. And, even if she was willing to come with me, a citizen's arrest wasn't going to fly. Not with her claiming I planted the gun, which she was sure to do. If she was willing to accuse me of it when she thought I was a cop, she was damn sure to accuse me of it when she found out I was a murder suspect.

I had to let her off the hook. But I had to do it very carefully so it didn't seem suspicious.

"I should really take you in," I said.

"Please."

She stood up, took a step toward me. Her sash was untied. She shrugged her shoul-

138

ders. The kimono fell to the floor.

Her breasts were full, her nipples pink and perky. She'd had a bikini wax since the picture.

And, as Mike Hammer would say, she was not a real blonde.

She reached her hands out toward me.

"Get dressed," I said.

She was shocked. She clearly couldn't believe it. What was I, gay?

"You're taking me in?"

"Put your robe on."

"What?"

I pointed to the kimono. "Go on. Put it on."

"You're *not* taking me in?"

"Put your robe on."

She picked up the kimono, slipped it on, knotted the sash.

"You just made a bad move," I told her. "I don't really think you're involved. Then you pull a bonehead play like that, that makes me think you are. Well, grow up, sister. It doesn't matter how cute and spunky you are, or what a great bod. If the bullets from this gun match the one that killed your boyfriend, not a lot's gonna help. By rights, I should make sure you're in custody when that happens. But, strictly speaking, a judge isn't going to issue an arrest warrant unless the bullets actually match. Technically, I gotta test the gun first. That gives you a narrow window of opportunity. An opportunity to do something smart and stop acting so damn dumb. You work tomorrow?"

"Yeah."

"Go to work. Go about your business. Do everything you would normally do. If I need you, I'll know where to find you. If things work out, I won't need you."

I sighed, shook my head.

"I know I'm going to regret this," I said.

I picked up the gun and walked out.

23

Alice couldn't believe it.

"Are you out of your mind?"

"She was naked. She had a gun."

"So you brought it to me?"

"I thought it might set a precedent."

"What?"

"Naked women with guns."

"Stanley."

"What was I supposed to do? There I was, impersonating a police officer, which they tend to frown on, suddenly the broad has a gun."

"Suddenly? I thought you found it in her trunk."

"I did."

"Then there was no 'suddenly' about it. It was a known gun, a premeditated gun. It wasn't sudden."

"Okay, the naked woman was sudden."

"I'll bet."

"I didn't ask her to take off the robe, Alice."

"No. You just implied you'd let her go if she did."

"I did nothing of the sort."

"Did she take off the robe?"

"Yes."

"Did you let her go?"

"That's not the point."

"What's the point?"

"I was letting her go anyway. I was never actually going to arrest her. You will recall I am not a cop."

"There's no need to shout."

"I wasn't shouting."

"You raised your voice."

"I'm stressed. I have dead bodies that I can't account for that are connected to me. That tends to make me edgy."

"Hadn't noticed. So, you had no intention of arresting this woman because you weren't a cop?"

"What are you getting at?"

"Did she know that?"

"Alice."

"If she didn't know that, the fact you couldn't have done it doesn't apply. As far as this woman knew, you were going to run her in."

"What's your point?"

"No point. Just trying to clarify the situation. Stanley, this isn't like you. Impersonating a police officer. Tampering with evidence."

"Who said I was a police officer? And how do I know the gun's evidence?"

"It's probably the murder weapon."

"No, it isn't."

"How can you be so sure?"

"She told me it wasn't."

"She was probably lying."

"She *was* lying. I caught her in it. Made her confess."

"Confess what?"

"She said she didn't know anything about the gun, I must have planted it on her. When I proved that wasn't true she admitted the gun was her boyfriend's and he must have loaned it to her and not taken it back."

"She admitted that?"

"Yes."

"But she didn't admit shooting her boyfriend with it while it was in her possession?"

"She didn't do that."

"What was she wearing when she told you she didn't do that?"

"Now you're just being silly."

"Right. You catch the woman in a lie and

143

she takes her clothes off. What does that tell you?"

"I should try to catch you in a lie?"

"Stop it, Stanley. I'm scared. You're charged with murder. It's ridiculous. We know that, but the cops don't. And then you run around making it worse. You find a body, you don't report it to the police. You find a murder weapon, you don't turn it in."

"How could I turn it in? They'd have arrested me for the second murder."

"Exactly. You're acting suicidal. If you wanted to get convicted you couldn't do a better job."

"I didn't *know* I was going to find a body. I didn't *know* I was going to find a gun."

"You knew you were going to find a gun after you found a gun."

"What?"

"You found a gun. In the trunk of a car. Did you drop it like it was red hot and get the hell out of there? No, you went to the bimbo's apartment and got it."

"My fingerprints were on it."

"Right. And wiping your fingerprints off it and putting it back in the trunk would have been much more dangerous than going to the woman's apartment, impersonating a police officer, and taking possession of what, if not the murder weapon, was at least a

144

gun in the possession of one of the chief suspects."

"She's not a chief suspect."

"No, you are. At least as far as the police are concerned. I'd expect you to know better."

"Oh, come on."

"No, you come on. Who's a more likely suspect, you or her?"

"I didn't do it."

"Right. That should make her more likely. I find it strange you don't think so."

"You're just playing with words, Alice."

"I'm not playing. It's not a game. You're in trouble. What are you going to do about it?"

"I don't know."

24

Richard was worse that Alice. Which is hard, because I'm not married to Richard. But, even with that handicap, the man managed to reduce me to rubble. Of course, he has a law degree. But what's a law degree compared to Alice?

"You got the murder weapon?" Richard said.

"It's not the murder weapon."

"No, it's just a recently fired gun in the possession of the victim's girlfriend. Tell me, what percentage of homicides are husband-wife related?"

"She's not his wife."

"Oh, she's just a *girlfriend.* Then it couldn't *possibly* be the same motivation. Because they don't have that *slip of paper* that says 'I'm going to make you angry enough to shoot me.' "

"I don't think she did."

"Despite having a recently fired gun."

"I don't think it's that recently fired. Here, see for yourself."

"You'd like to get *my* fingerprints on it? Just in case yours aren't enough to get me charged as an accessory and get me disbarred."

"You're an attorney. No one's charging you with anything."

"Oh, attorneys are immune from the law. I forgot. Thank goodness I have you around to refresh my memory on some of these finer points."

"You haven't done anything wrong."

"Quoth the scofflaw. It was bad enough when you were just costing me money. Now you're going to cost me my entire practice."

"Right," I said, "it's all about you."

Richard closed his mouth. Glared at me. "Excuse me. I'm sorry. I was thinking of myself, when I should be thinking of my pro bono client. Who's gone out of his way to jeopardize my existence. I lost sight of my prime objective, saving you from your most recent series of bonehead moves."

"You see why I had to take the gun."

"Of course. So when the girlfriend identifies you as the guy who impersonated a cop, they'll know who to ask for it."

"Any time you're through kidding around."

"*I'm* kidding around? You think *I'm* kidding around? I'm not kidding around. I'm stalling while I try to figure out if I have to turn you in to the cops, and if I do, what do I tell them? I mean, Jesus Christ, can you think of a story that even *sounds* plausible?"

"No, I can't."

"Why are you here?"

"You're my attorney."

"Not by choice. You got me in a position where I can't withdraw my services without forfeiting twenty-five grand and risking going to jail."

"You're taking this personally again."

"What, like *The Godfather,* it's not personal, it's just business? Well, guess what? When they nail me for my part in this, who do you think will be doing time? My business? You think Wendy and Janet will pull a few months for me?"

"Richard."

"This is not a slap-on-the-wrist crime here. This is a situation where a suspended sentence would seem like a win."

"I don't see what's so bad."

"You can't search crime scenes. You can't appropriate murder weapons."

"It wasn't a crime scene when I searched it."

"Why, because there wasn't a ribbon? You

148

got there ahead of the police. You know how much worse that is?"

"Yesterday's news, Richard. You already bawled me out for that."

"Right. You didn't find anything at the crime scene, so you went out and got me a gun."

I'd actually found a body at the crime scene, but it didn't seem like a good time to bring it up. "What did you want me to do with the gun? I couldn't leave it with her. It had my fingerprints on it."

"What? Someone put your fingerprints on it? Then of course you're not to blame."

"I was searching the woman's car. I found a gun. I didn't expect to find it. I put my hand in her purse and there it was. After I'd taken it out of her purse it would have been stupid not to see if it had been fired. It had, which was embarrassing."

"Embarrassing? What a wonderful way to put it. I framed myself for a murder. It's a little embarrassing."

"Which is why I had to retrieve it. I not only had my fingerprints on the gun, I had my fingerprints on the bullets."

"I understand that. What I don't understand is why you had to bring it to me."

"You'd prefer I didn't tell you what I was doing?"

"I'd prefer you didn't *do* it. Look at the position you put me in. I either have to turn it in to the police and risk being disbarred for betraying the confidence of a client. Or not turn it in to the police and be disbarred for compounding a felony and conspiring to conceal a crime."

"What crime? The gun wasn't used in a crime. It's got nothing to do with anything."

"And you actually believe that."

"The woman told me that."

"And she seemed very sincere."

The image of her dropping the robe came to mind. I tried to keep my face neutral. I shouldn't have bothered. Not with the demon interrogator.

Richard poked a finger in my face. "Aha! Something is bothering you. In your assessment of the sincerity of her statement. What makes you think she's lying?"

"I don't think she's lying."

"Then what is it?"

I told him about Jersey Girl taking her clothes off.

Richard rolled his eyes. "A moron. I'm dealing with a moron. The woman's story is so bad she offers you her body to believe it. Tell me, when she offered you her body, did she seem very sincere?"

"That doesn't mean she's lying."

"No, she could be demented. She could be the type of woman who takes her clothes off just to ease the strain of social situations."

"I didn't mention she took her clothes off because I was afraid you wouldn't be able to get around it. She was naked, she looked good, I was grateful for the show. Not so grateful I'd cover up a murder."

"That's just what you're doing."

"Only if the gun is the murder weapon. And I don't think it is."

"Now you don't *think* it is? A moment ago, with visions of bare breasts dancing in your head you were sure it wasn't."

"I'm sure it isn't. If it isn't, I've done nothing wrong." Richard was about jump in. I pushed on. "At least nothing that should concern the police."

"And if it is the murder weapon, you're aiding and abetting a felon. In the eyes of the law, the yeah-but-I-did't-think-so defense has never been successfully raised. That's why you don't put yourself in the position where you have to make that value judgment."

"Yeah, but since I am, the gun is either the murder weapon or it isn't. I take the position that it isn't. Until someone proves that it is, I've done nothing wrong."

"Yes. And the flip side is, when they do, you go to jail."

"It would be nice to prove conclusively that I'm right."

"It would be nice to win the lottery. I don't expect it to happen, but it would certainly be nice."

"Come on, Richard, just because you're pissed at me doesn't mean you can't help. If I've really put you in such a bad position I would think you'd want to get out of it."

"I'd love to get out of it. You just seem hell bent on making it impossible."

"What do you want me to do?"

"I'd love for you to do nothing, but that's like wishing for the moon. You've made such a mess of things it's hard to know where to start." Richard sighed. "Practicing law would be so easy if there weren't any clients."

Good. Richard was almost through beating me up and was slipping into lecture mode. Soon he might calm down enough to offer some advice. Or be willing to listen to some.

"About the gun," I said. I hated to bring it up again, but it was the reason I came.

Richard looked at me as if I'd committed some social blunder by mentioning a taboo subject. "What about it?"

"It would be really nice if we could prove it had nothing to do with the crime."

"Too bad we can't."

"Well, that's the thing. If we could figure out a way to get a photograph of the fatal bullet —"

Richard exploded from his desk. "I don't believe it! There's no stopping you. Why bother with a jury trial? Why don't you just confess?"

"Richard."

"You're not *charged* with this crime. Nothing *connects* you to this crime. As far as the police know, the two crimes have nothing to do with each other. But you want to hand them a connection readymade. Do you know what that means? That means I can't plea bargain. In a worst-case scenario, if they wanted to get you for, say, obstruction of justice, in the first murder, I can't take it, because then they'll turn around and try you for the second. And they'll be able to use the conviction from the first against you. In the second there will *be* no plea bargain, because they'll be trying a convicted felon."

"Richard —"

"And after they convict you the second time — and if they get you for anything the first time they damn well will the second time — that's when they turn around and come after me. Though I certainly apologize from mentioning it in the midst of a conversation that is entirely about you."

"Are you saying it can't be done, or are you saying it's inadvisable to try to do it?"

He shook his head. "Unbelievable."

"Richard, I know it's bad. That's why I'm trying so desperately to get out of it. Everything I do seems to make it worse, but not doing anything seems suicidal. Not that I don't think you're going to do a crackerjack job defending me. But I don't expect these cops to come up with any shred of evidence that doesn't point to me."

"I know," Richard said. "It's your storybook mentality. If I get you off, it won't be good enough, because I didn't find out who did it. Well, guess what? This is very likely one of those crimes that is never solved. Getting you off is the optimal result."

"I know that."

"I know you know that. The problem is you don't act like you know that. Or you wouldn't be asking me to get ahold of the fatal bullet."

"Not the fatal bullet. Just a photograph of the fatal bullet."

"I understand the concept. And it's not gonna happen. Or I'm gonna get my bail bond back and put you in jail where you can't get into any more trouble."

"Can you do that?"

"It's my money. I put it up. If I wanna surrender you and get it back, who's gonna stop me?"

I wasn't sure if Richard could actually do that or if he was bluffing, but it didn't seem like a good time to find out.

"I'm kind of happy being on bail. Whaddya say we keep the status quo?"

"And you'll stop hassling me about the fatal bullet?"

"Sure thing, Richard. What do you want me to do with the gun?"

Richard rolled his eyes. "Oh, my, what a straight line." His face hardened. "I want you to do absolutely nothing with the gun. I want you to take the gun out of here and forget you ever showed it to me. Because I certainly intend to. In the very unlikely event it becomes necessary to worry about the gun, we will worry about it then. But, until such a time, I would prefer to pretend that it doesn't exist. Is that agreeable to you?"

"Sure."

"And you will cease and desist in attempting to match any bullets from it with any bullets from any known felonies?"

"I promise."

25

In MacAullif's case, I led with Jersey Girl taking her clothes off. I figured it was the only thing that would keep him from throwing me out of his office. I figured right. He was coming around his desk just as I got to her dropping her robe. He broke stride, said, "What was she wearing underneath?"

"Nothing?"

"She was naked?"

"As a jaybird."

"Fuck the jaybird. What did she look like?"

"Prominent nipples. Dark and pointed. She recently had a bikini wax."

"She spread her legs?"

"MacAullif."

"Just asking."

"She was standing up."

"And?"

"What do you mean, 'and'?"

"What happened then?"

"Nothing happened then. She was trying

to distract me from what was going on."

"What *was* going on?"

"Nothing was going on. I was just questioning her about her relationship with the decedent."

"What was that?"

"She was his girlfriend."

"Full time?"

"She wasn't living with him."

"She seem broken up?"

"Not particularly. She went right back to work."

"What's she do?"

"She's a hairdresser."

"With big tits?"

"It's a prerequisite."

"And why were you questioning her?"

"Why don't you sit down."

"Why?"

"Keeps you calm. Sit down, play with a couple of cigars. Make you feel better."

"I feel just fine."

"Make *me* feel better."

"And why don't you feel well?"

"Are you kidding me? I'm a defendant in a murder case."

"No, why would you feel better about me sitting down?"

"Did you see yourself coming around the desk? If this girl hadn't happened to be nude I would probably be dead."

"You gonna tell me why she took her clothes off?"

"If you want me to speculate on women's motivations. I mean, who knows why they do what they do."

"From your evasion this must be pretty bad."

"Well, it's not good."

"I'm on a new blood pressure medication. I haven't really had a chance to test it."

"I'm glad to be of help."

"I'm not amused. What did you do that's so bad you want me sitting down when I hear it?"

"Why don't you sit down and I'll tell you?"

MacAullif took a deep breath, exhaled slowly through his teeth. It sounded somewhat like a steam engine. He marched around his desk and plunked himself in his chair. "Okay. Shoot."

"Funny you should say that."

I resisted the temptation to pull the gun. Instead, as gently as possible, I broke the news to MacAullif of my latest adventure into the realm of the absurd.

Needless to say he wasn't thrilled. "You impersonated a police officer and appropriated a murder weapon?"

"I didn't impersonate anybody. I wore a

suit and said 'we'. If the woman thought I was a cop, that's hardly my fault."

"Bullshit. What reason did you give her for taking the gun?"

"I told her it needed to be tested in order to determine if it was used in the shooting. Which happens to be true."

"What excuse did you give for not taking her in?"

"It was a favor for showing me her tits."

"I'm serious."

"So am I. I didn't say that, but that's the way she read it."

"I should turn you in."

"Yeah, but you can't. It's the fruit of the poisonous tree. I got onto her because she's the girlfriend of the guy whose address you got me from the motel. So there's nothing you can do."

MacAullif shook his head. "If it's a murder weapon, I gotta turn it in."

"Yeah, but it's not. A girl with nice tits and a bikini wax told me it's not, and I tend to believe her. On the other hand, if that should turn out to be a faulty assumption, something would have to be done."

MacAullif's eyes narrowed. "Why are you here?"

"To bring you up to date."

"You don't want me up to date. The last

time you brought me up to date you wound up stranded on the Palisades Parkway. The only reason you'd be here is if you want something. So what do you want this time?"

"Will you stay seated?"

MacAullif groaned. "Let me guess. You want me to get ahold of the fatal bullet and see if it came from this gun."

"Now that you mention it."

"Not going to happen," MacAullif said. He seemed remarkably calm. "It's not going to happen because it would be suicidal. For a number of reasons which I'm sure your attorney already told you. And here you are, disregarding his advice, asking me anyway. Or perhaps, acting against his explicit instructions might be more accurate."

"MacAullif."

"What did Richard say when you showed him the gun?"

"I didn't say I showed him the gun."

"If you hadn't, you wouldn't be here. Your attorney's your first line of defense. Unless you've already disobeyed so many of his instructions you don't dare talk to him either. I don't think I've ever seen anybody dig a deeper hole. I mean, you're doing a routine surveillance. Husband-wife thing, what can possibly go wrong? Best case

161

scenario you have something to report, so the client doesn't think she wasted her money. Worst case scenario you sit there all night and nothing happens. Your client may think you're an incompetent douchebag, but she can't prove it, and you still get paid. But not in your wildest dreams is the end result you get charged with a homicide and stuck covering up another."

"So you're not going to do it?"

MacAullif sighed. "It's like talking to the wall. No, I'm not going to do it. I'm going to live out my few years until retirement in relative peace and contentment. I'm going to hope that in that time no one comes around asking me embarrassing questions that get me booted off the force. But if they do, so be it, it will serve me right for trying to do a favor for a friend."

"You don't know anybody from the Jersey Shore?"

MacAullif came out of his chair. "Are you deaf? Are you willfully stupid? You put yourself in a position where nothing is going to help. You gotta bail. Cut your losses. Live to play another day. Taking this gun has to be the stupidest thing you've ever done, and I don't care how many tits you got to see. If I were you I would polish that gun as free of fingerprints as it can be, put

162

it in an equally fingerprint-free carton, and mail it to the cops."

"You're kidding."

"Safest thing to do. Solves all your problems. If it isn't the murder weapon, it won't matter a bit. If it is the murder weapon, you'll find out."

"That's not a bad idea."

"Damn straight. Is there anything else I could do for you?"

"You sure you don't know any officers on the Jersey Shore?"

I was out the door before MacAullif made it around the desk.

26

It was a one-story building of mortar and brick, not the most imposing edifice in the world. The neon sign out front that said Police could just as easily have said Diner or Motel. I walked in the front door, found myself in an outer office where a single cop in uniform manned a cluttered desk. There was a counter along one wall, and a corridor leading to various inner offices and/or holding cells.

The cop at the desk looked up. "Can I help you?"

"You have some evidence for Sergeant Fuller, Ft. Lee."

The cop, who gave the impression he was used to being given the runaround by plainclothes cops, heaved a sigh. "No one told me about it."

"Figures. I knew you wouldn't know. But just try talking back, huh? I mean, something like this you could fax it, right? Or email it as an attachment. As a gif or a tiff or a jpeg. You know, anyone could do it. Well, I couldn't do it, but my wife could. But, no, people do it this way because they've always done it this way. So I gotta drive down here. They could at least tell you so you had it ready."

"Had what ready?"

"Photo of the fatal bullet."

"What fatal bullet?"

"Oh, for Christ's sake. Hang on, I got it written down." I fished a notebook out of my jacket pocket, riffled through it. "Here we go. Vinnie Carbone. Apparently it's a homicide."

"Oh, yeah. It's a homicide, all right."

"So you got it?"

"No one told me about this."

"I'm not surprised."

"I gotta call somebody."

"Who?"

"I don't know. Let's see, who caught this one?"

There was a microphone on the desk. He pulled it to him, pressed a button. "Hey, Sammy?" he said, and released the button.

A moment later the radio crackled. "Yeah?"

"Vinnie Carbone case."

"What about it?"

"Is that your case?"

"Fred Seager's lead."

"Guy from Ft. Lee wants to see the fatal bullet."

"Come again?"

"Guy from Ft. Lee wants a photograph of the fatal bullet."

"Why?"

"See if there's any connection to a case he's got there."

"So give it to him."

"Where is it?"

"Huh?"

"Where's the photograph?"

"You'll have to ask Fred."

"He won't be in till tonight."

"Ask him tonight."

"Guy's here now."

"So call over to the lab. They should have copies."

The cop released the microphone, picked up the phone.

"I appreciate this," I said.

The cop shrugged. "Just routine."

The door banged open and two plainclothes cops came in. I knew they were cops because they were dressed like me, and they acted bored. The taller, wirier of the two barged right by the desk without so much as a second glance. His partner, short and fat, threw the cop at the desk a nod. A rookie mistake, it gave the guy the chance to pass the buck.

"Hey, Charlie," he called. "You guys know anything about the Vinnie Carbone case?"

The tall cop turned back. "What about it?"

"Cop in Ft. Lee's asking. Wants to see the fatal bullet."

"Oh, does he now?" The tall cop, who seemed to have a chip on his shoulder, fixed his eyes on me. "Who are you?"

I put up my hands. "Hey, don't look at me. Sergeant Fuller wants to see the bullet. Not the bullet. Photo of the bullet. I'm here to pick it up."

"Why are you here to pick it up?"

"You think Fuller's gonna drive down himself?"

"What's his angle?"

"He's got his own murder case."

"I thought he got the guy who did it."

"He made bail."

"Really? Fuckin' system. Well, good luck getting your picture."

"What do you mean?"

"You wouldn't believe the red tape."

"Christ, yes," the fat cop said. "Remember when we had to get that gun from Trenton?"

"What gun from Trenton?"

"It was the murder weapon here, but they didn't want to surrender it because it was used in an armed robbery there."

"Oh, right."

"Same thing here. Nobody's gonna hand over the murder weapon."

The wheels were starting to come off, the fabrication spinning out of control. "But there was no murder weapon here," I said. "Just a bullet. Fuller's got the murder weapon. The point was to see whether the bullet down here came from it."

"He thinks the crimes are related?"

"He doesn't think the crimes are related. There's no reason to think the crimes are related. The only conceivable reason to think the crimes are related is to ruin my afternoon by making me drive down here to prove that they're not." I put up my hands again. "Sorry. Don't mean to get upset. It's just the mountains of bullshit they make you swim through. Not you guys. The system."

"You work with Fuller?"

"That's not that way I'd phrase it."

The tall cop seemed amused. "What do you think of him?"

I shrugged. "Guy's a bit of a dickhead."

Tall cop laughed. "Hey, Rick," he said to the guy at the desk. "What you say you help our buddy here out."

"What do you mean?"

"Call the lab, see if they got the photo he wants. If they do, tell 'em Sergeant Stark wants it and you're sending a detective to pick it up. They'll give it to you if they think it's for me. Another county, they'll make a fuss."

"Thanks, man."

"Don't thank me yet. They may not have it."

I should have let that go. I couldn't help myself. "Why not?"

"There's no gun. They got a gun, they're firing test bullets, comparing them, having a grand old time. If there's nothing to compare it with, it isn't urgent. Unless someone's specifically asking, there's no rush getting it done."

Rick hung up the phone. "They got it. They'll hold it for you at the desk."

I got in the car with mixed feelings. I'd expedited getting the photo. But I'd met far more New Jersey policemen than could possibly be good for my health.

At least I hadn't had to give them a name.

27

The crime lab in Trenton was in the top floor of a four-story office building in midtown with no place to park. I cruised around, found a parking meter three blocks down. It was a half-hour meter of all things, but how long could this possibly take? Nonetheless, I stepped along briskly on my way to the lab.

Good thing I did. The cop at the desk, who was supposed to have my photo, looked at me as if I were a creature from another planet.

"I'm here to pick up a photo of the fatal bullet in the Vinnie Carbone case. I was told it would be at the desk."

"Who told you that?"

"Rick. The desk cop. He called over to make sure."

"And who are you?"

"I'm picking up the photo for Sergeant Stark."

"Uh huh." The cop had a computer on his desk. He typed into it. Shook his head. "Not his case."

"I know it's not his case. He just wants to see the bullet."

"Why?"

"He didn't say. He asked me to pick up the photo. He had Rick call over here to make sure there wouldn't be a problem."

"And who are you?" he repeated.

I wasn't sure which was worse, giving my name, or making one up. But if Fuller got wind of this, the name Hastings would be a red flag. "Hailey," I said. "And what's your name?"

That caught him up short. "Why?"

"If Stark doesn't get his photo I need to know who to refer him to."

There went my last chance of ever being his friend. The not-so-veiled-threat jarred him out of his smug complacency. "Hold on here. I didn't say you can't have the photo. Before I give anything out I want to make damn sure who it's going to."

"It's going to Sergeant Stark. He was under the impression you'd give him anything he wanted."

"Him, I would. You I don't know from Adam."

"So call Rick."

That had him stymied. It was clearly the thing to do, but he didn't want to do it because it was my suggestion. He reluctantly picked up the phone and punched in the number. "Rick Daniels? . . . Oh? Where is he? . . . Hi, Sy. Listen, what do you know about some photo for Sergeant Stark? . . . How the hell should I know what photo? Guy here says Stark sent him to pick it up. Detective — what's your name again?"

"Hailey."

"Detective Hailey . . . You never heard of him? Well, that's hardly a ringing endorsement. Hang on. . . ." The cop cupped the mouthpiece with some satisfaction. "They know nothing about it and they never heard of you."

"Of course not. I spoke to Stark and Daniels. You're talking to the wrong guys."

"I don't care who I'm talking to. They don't know you from Adam."

Uh oh. I could feel my knees getting weak. Envisioned handcuffs being clamped on my wrists. The expression "caught red-handed" came to mind.

I stuck out my chin. "What's the matter," I said. "Didn't they take the photo?"

That caught him off guard. "Huh?"

"Stark told me it would be like that. They got no gun so there's no rush on the fatal

172

bullet. They may not have even taken the pictures yet."

He glowered at me. "Who the hell you think you are, walk in here, throw around charges like that?"

"Sergeant tells me to pick up the picture, they even call ahead to make sure it's okay. Not only is it *not* okay, the way you're acting I don't think they even got a picture of the bullet."

A technical-looking type came out the other door. I know that's stereotyping, but the guy had on what could have passed for scrubs if they had been a different shade, and he was carrying his hands as if he had just washed them and was heading into an operating room, though he obviously wasn't.

"Maybe you know," I said. "You know anything about the pictures of the Vinnie Carbone bullet?"

He smiled. "Who are you?"

Why did everyone have to ask me that? "I'm Detective Hailey. Sergeant Stark wants a photo of the fatal bullet." '

"Why, did he find the gun?"

"He didn't say."

"You talk to him in person?"

"Yeah."

"Then he must not have found a gun, or he'd have sent it over."

"You have the photo?"

"Not my department." He looked at the cop at the desk. "You know anything about this?"

"Just what you do. Guy waltzes in here, wants the evidence, doesn't want to give anything in return."

I couldn't help asking. "What do you want in return?"

He shrugged. "I don't know. Sandwich would be nice. Brisket on white with lettuce and mayo."

My mouth fell open. The guy had to be pulling my leg. I mean, wasn't he?

The technician said, "Lemme see if Charlie knows anything about this."

"Thanks. I sure don't," the desk cop said.

The technician went back the way he came.

I wandered around looking at the walls, hoping to distract the cop from asking me any more questions. Luckily, he didn't seem to give a damn. With the technician taking over, it was no longer his problem, no skin off his nose.

The good news was the technician was back in minutes.

The bad news was his hands were empty.

"Wally says it's not Stark's case."

"Yeah, I know. Stark just wanted to see it."

"Well, Wally made a copy, left it at the desk."

The cop at the desk said, "He didn't leave it with me."

"Right," I said, rather testily. "He left it with the other guy. So where is it?"

The cop's chin came up. "Hey, you want it or not?"

"I want it, I want it. Jeez, such a simple thing, suddenly it's a federal case. So, where would he have left it?"

"I have no idea."

"How about that manila envelope in the Out basket?"

I picked it up, turned it over.

It said "Stark."

"There you go," I said.

The cop looked at me. "Just cause it says 'Stark' doesn't mean anything. You want me to turn it over to you, I need some identification."

I had no identification in the name of Hailey. Even if I did, it wouldn't have identified me as a police officer. I eyed the door, weighed my chances if I ran for it. They were not good. Even if I made it to my car, they'd be sure to get the license number.

While I was thinking that, the cop picked

175

up the manila envelope, unclasped the prongs, and opened the flap. He reached in, pulled out an eight-by-ten color photograph showing the striations on a bullet.

"I guess that's it," it said.

He shoved it back in the envelope, closed the flap, and handed it to me.

28

The ballistics expert wasn't happy. "You're not a cop?"

"No."

"And you want me to compare a bullet?"

"I want you to fire a bullet through this gun, compare it to the bullet in this picture."

The photo was an edited version of the one I'd gotten from the lab. The heading with the case, name, number, and jurisdiction had been cut off, as had the signature of the lab technician who had taken the photograph. In my humble opinion they were not necessary. After all, I was only dealing with one bullet.

"I'm studying forensics. I have a homework assignment on identifying bullets."

"And you want me to do it for you?"

"I don't have the equipment. I need a picture on a comparison microscope. I'll write the paper."

"But you want me to line up the bullet so

it matches."

"Not at all. I want you to compare the bullet and tell me *if* it matches. If it does, I'll have a lot to write. If it doesn't, I'll have a lot to write, it just won't be as easy."

"You think the bullet will match?"

"Frankly, I think it won't. But I need a comparison to write the paper around. Can you do it?"

The expert was younger than I would have expected, but then everyone is these days. He cocked his head, said, "All bullshit aside, what's the story here?"

"What do you mean?"

"This bullet came from a police lab." He put up his hands. "Not that there's anything wrong with that. They use them in education. But they leave the headers on. So you know what you're dealing with. This photo's been mutilated. Which means something isn't kosher."

"It's a blind test. One student is given a fatal gun and a fatal bullet. Everyone else is given a placebo." I wondered if you could say that in forensics, or just in medical trials.

"Doesn't that give one student an incredible advantage?"

"Yes, if it were true. I think they lied to us. I think either all of the bullets match, or none of them do."

"Aren't you a little old to be taking a forensics course?"

"Thank you very much."

"You mind telling me what's really going on?"

I sighed. Whipped out my ID. "Look. I have this gun. I need to know if it fired this bullet. If it did, I'll have to get the police involved. But I don't want to involve them if it didn't."

He considered. "Okay. Two hundred bucks and I'll have it by tomorrow."

"I need it now."

"Yeah, well, you can't have it now. I gotta fire the gun, make the comparison photos, type up a report."

"I don't need a report. I just need a yes or no answer, is it the gun?"

"I understand. And I can't give you a snap answer. If you'd actually had a course in forensics you'd know this was precision work."

"Can't you tell right away if it wasn't the gun?"

He shook his head. "Gun's a .38. Bullet is too. Class characteristics are going to match. So you're talking individual characteristics. It's a tricky thing. And if this is as important as you say, it better be right."

"It's as important as I say."

"Then maybe you better have it done in a police lab."

"Fine," I said. "Tomorrow would be great."

I got the hell out of there so as not to prolong the conversation. Believe me, I wasn't happy. Waiting till the next day was going to be excruciating. I was afraid I'd walk into the guy's office tomorrow and he'd say, "There's no doubt, the bullet came from the gun."

But that far from the worst-case scenario.

The worst-case scenario was I'd walk into his office and it would be filled with cops. Whom he'd called as soon as he got me out of his office. Which is *why* he got me out of his office. I mean, come on, the guy's an expert, he can't compare a bullet while I wait? The more I thought of it, the more it seemed a likely premise. Would he have called the New York cops, or would he have called the New Jersey cops? The guy had recognized the photo as coming from a crime lab. Could he tell which crime lab? "Oh, yeah, that's the type of photographic paper they use in Jersey." And if he called the Jersey cops, would Fuller be one of them? Wanting to know what the hell a gun and bullet had to do with his homicide, at which he'd recovered the gun and bullet.

No, finding cops in the ballistics expert's office would be about as ugly as it could get. But aside from that, finding the bullet matched would be a hell of a kick in the crotch. Assuming that happened, I would be one mighty unhappy detective.

I figured I better prepare for that possibility.

29

I staked out the beauty parlor at three in the afternoon. I tried staking out Jersey Girl's home but she wasn't there. I checked out the beauty parlor on a hunch, figuring she might work different shifts. She did, and she was there, and I staked her out.

Frankly, I didn't expect to learn anything by staking out Jersey Girl, but I was scared to death of what I might miss by not staking out Jersey Girl. So, there I was, once again, watching the beauty parlor with high anxiety and low expectations.

She was out a 4:35. That was a break. I was afraid she'd stay until eight. I started the car, fully prepared to follow her home.

Only she didn't go home. She cruised around a few streets, and got on the New Jersey Turnpike heading south. She went two exits, got off, and drove out to where the residential properties looked lush.

Jersey Girl parked in the street beside a

sprawling, two-story frame house with a flashy-looking car in the drive. She walked up the concrete path to the front stoop and rang the bell. She must have been impatient, because it seemed only a second before she rang it again.

The door was opened by a teenager with an attitude. In my day we'd have said "bad attitude," but today we say "attitude" to mean "bad attitude," which seems unfair to the word, but then who am I to judge? The kid must have been right at that fine line where computer games still trumped computer porn, because lush Jersey Girl might have been a wet dishrag to him. He shut the door in her face, went back inside.

Jersey Girl stood there a few moments, then turned and came down off the stoop. I thought she was leaving, but then she hesitated, looked over her shoulder toward the house. She seemed lost, helpless.

The front door banged open and a woman came out. She might have been attractive but she had her hair in curlers and a scarf on her head. I couldn't hear her, but it didn't take a genius to figure out what she was saying. The woman clearly didn't like Jersey Girl. In fact, a catfight was not out of the question. That seemed a little harsh, with a woman whose boyfriend was recently dead. Anyway, Curler Head stepped up and went went jaw to jaw with Jersey Girl.

Jersey Girl wasn't about to take it lying down. Yes, I realized what that sounded like the moment I thought it. But you know what I mean. She strode up to Curler Head as if she were about to give her a permanent without benefit of anesthetic. Then, in a perfectly-timed anticlimax, she turned on her heel, marched down the sidewalk to her car, and drove off.

I was late getting started. Partly because I wanted to give Curler Head time to get inside so she wouldn't notice the co-incidence of two cars pulling out at the same time, and partly because Jersey Girl was so quick she caught me by surprise.

At any rate, I lost her.

I sure hoped I wouldn't have to explain how that happened to Alice, MacAullif, Richard, or any number of New Jersey cops.

I headed for the Jersey Turnpike, since that was how we came, got on, and drove like the devil. I didn't see her anywhere. I got off and drove straight to her house.

She wasn't there.

Proving, as if I needed any further proof, that I am not cut out for this job.

She showed up half an hour later. Hardly enough time to have gotten into any trouble.

Long enough to convince me she probably had.

She parked and went into her house.

I weighed my options. I could go inside and ask her where she'd been. Or I could jump into the mouth of an active volcano.

It was a toss-up.

30

I called MacAullif, gave him the address of the house.

He didn't sound happy. "What about it?"

"Who lives there?"

"You're in no position to be asking any favors."

"You're in no position to be refusing."

"What the hell are you talking about?"

"Remember the thing that was bad?"

"Yeah."

"Well, it's worse."

"How could it be worse?"

"Think about it."

"You did something stupid?"

"Would that surprise you?"

"Yes, it would. You're in so much trouble any move you make could be fatal. That should be apparent to even you."

"Forget it, MacAullif. We're way beyond that. I got a lead. The guy who lives at this address could be pay dirt."

"What makes you think so?"

"His wife doesn't like the widow."

"What widow?"

"Jersey Girl."

"The one you stole the gun from?"

"Is this a secure line?"

"Yeah, right. Like the department bugs my calls. Listen, dipshit, I don't know what you're up to, but you're all out of favors. You don't want me to slam down the phone, start making sense."

"Jersey Girl rang the front doorbell. Apparently the man of the house wasn't home, because his wife came out and tried to rip her tits off."

"A cat fight?"

"Not really. All talk and no action."

"That's disappointing."

"Can you find out who the guy is?"

"Why?"

"I'd like to know if he killed her boyfriend because he's hot for her bod."

"You've got the guy's address. Why don't you look him up yourself?"

"I'd like more than his name."

"Like what?"

"I'd like to know if he's in the mob."

"Oh, great."

"One more thing."

"One more thing? You ask me to trace a

mobster, and you want one more thing?"

"You'll like this. Jersey Girl. The naked girl. The girl with the nice tits."

"What about her?"

"Wouldn't you like to know who she is?"

"Don't you know?"

"She lives over someone's garage. It's not that easy to trace. But I got her license plate number." I took out my notebook, read it to him. "Could you run it?"

"Just in case I get curious," MacAullif said sarcastically. "Thank you so much."

"My pleasure."

"So, what did you do with the gun?"

"I've still got it."

"You hesitated before you said that. Is that because you're lying?"

"Wanna see it?"

"I most definitely do *not* wanna see it. I wanna maintain plausible deniability. You remember me telling you if you had any gun I didn't know about, it would behoove you to get rid of it?"

"Do cops actually say 'behoove'?"

"Hey, asshole."

"I'll get rid of it, I'll get rid of it." Visions of the ballistics expert danced in my head. "What's the extradition agreement between New York and New Jersey?"

"Extradition?"

"If I get arrested in New York, and I'm wanted in Jersey, do I have to go?"

"Doesn't matter."

"Why not?"

"You'll be there before you can raise the point."

"I have my lawyer on speed dial."

"Ever dial a phone with your hands cuffed behind your back?"

"Can't say as I have."

"Better practice."

31

"It's definitely from the same gun."

"You're kidding!"

The ballistics expert shook his head. "There's no doubt about it. Here, look at these pictures from the comparison microscope. See how the striations line up? Here's an enlargement. You see that?"

I didn't. I had stopped looking, stopped listening. My head was coming off. All my worst dreams were coming true. Well, there weren't cops in his office, but aside from that. I gave the guy his two hundred bucks and got the hell out of there.

I had to get rid of the gun. That was one thing MacAullif said that made sense. And he didn't even know it was the murder weapon. As far as he was concerned, it would merely seal the deal on impersonating an officer. He didn't know it would make me an accomplice after the fact to murder.

The charges were really piling up.

Which put me in a horrible position. I couldn't keep it, and I couldn't get rid of it.

By rights, I should give it back to Jersey Girl. Then the cops could catch her with it and prosecute her for it. Only they couldn't anymore, because I'd taken it away from her. And who was to say the one I gave her back was the same one she gave me?

That was just for starters. Even if I had given her back the same one she gave me, I was still impersonating an officer when I did it. And by doing that, I had probably fucked up the evidence so badly that she could never be prosecuted, though I certainly could.

So the only way to give it back to her was to give it back to her without her knowledge. Plant it in her car, for instance. Only that wouldn't work, because she would still tell people about the police officer who took her gun. She would claim he must have planted the gun on her. Which was what she was telling me to begin with, only this time it would be true. True, but irrelevant, since planting the gun was only to put things back the way they were to begin with, and maintain the status quo.

I wondered if I should do that.

I wondered if I should drive back to Jersey.

I wondered if I should *walk* back to Jersey and drop the gun in the Hudson River from the middle of the George Washington Bridge.

I stopped in at the Westside Stationery Store and bought a manila mailer, the padded kind with the bubble wrap inside. I put the gun in it, sealed it up.

I went to the post office, got a Priority Mail label, addressed it to myself, General Delivery, Westport, Connecticut. I put my real address as the return address.

I went to the Priority Mail self-service machine where you can avoid the line by dipping your credit card and weighing it yourself.

I dipped my credit card, answered some questions. I lied to the machine. It asked me if I was mailing anything dangerous and I said no.

I pulled out the postage label, slapped it on the package, and dropped it in the bin.

I immediately felt a sense of relief, and it wasn't just that the pistol hadn't discharged when it hit the bottom. It wasn't loaded, but even so. Even an unloaded gun could have that one, stray shell in the chamber that blows your head off. Not this time. I walked out of the post office a free and unarmed man.

I stood on the sidewalk, took a deep breath. The sun was shining. It was a beautiful day.

I was totally screwed. I had taken a chance that Jersey Girl was an innocent victim of circumstance who just happened to have her boyfriend's gun. Instead she was a lying scheming murderess, which put my actions, always questionable, in a much less legal light. I had not impersonated a police officer to prove to my satisfaction that the girlfriend of the murdered man in fact had nothing to do with his demise. No, I had impersonated a police officer in order to suppress the murder weapon, making it next to impossible to convict the woman who was almost certainly guilty. I had a feeling the police would be apt to frown on that.

My cell phone rang. I nearly peed my pants. I was that wound up. I whipped it out (my cell phone), and flipped it open.

It was MacAullif.

"Tony Gallo."

"Huh?"

"The name you wanted. It's Tony Gallo."

"Oh."

"That's right. Runs a salvage company down by the docks. That's 'salvage company' in quotes. Tony Gallo is connected. In a big way. So big I don't even *have* to look him up. The guy's a mob boss. A notorious mob boss. With a rather nasty disposition."

"Great."

"Isn't it. So if that bare-titted broad you're infatuated with is involved with Tony Gallo, she'd be a hell of a good person to stay away from."

"I see."

"I ran her plate, by the way. She's Angela Russo. In case the name comes up, you'll know to run the other direction."

"Angela Russo."

"Christ, he's in love. I'm not kidding, here. The girl's living poison, you give her a wide berth."

"Yeah."

"You get rid of that gun?"

"Yes, I did."

"Good. Even if it's not the gun that killed her boyfriend, you want nothing to do with it. You want nothing to do with her. Just pretend she doesn't exist."

MacAullif hung up.

I flipped my cell phone shut.

Oh boy.

Jersey Girl's married boyfriend was Tony Gallo, and Tony Gallo was a mob boss, and not just any mob boss, but a mob boss so scary, MacAullif had not only warned me off him, but also off her. And that was without even knowing she had the gun that killed her boyfriend.

All right. This was it. I'd painted myself into a corner where I couldn't do anything because every move was bad.

Which was actually good. It didn't matter what I did, because any move was apt to be fatal.

So I could do anything.

32

Tony Gallo's "salvage company" listed an address in Newark. I cruised by. It was an empty lot.

The address had a phone number. I dialed it.

A voice answered with a Jersey twang. "Speak to me."

"Tony Gallo."

"Who's calling?"

"A friend."

"Then why don't I know you?"

"Are you Tony Gallo?"

"No."

"That's why."

There was a silence on the line. Small victory. If salvage meant what I thought it did, I'd bluffed out a wiseguy.

After a moment the voice said, "What do you want with Tony?"

"It's personal."

"Then call him at home."

"I can't call him at home."

"Why not?"

"It's personal. I need to have a talk with him without involving his wife."

"Hold on."

I waited half a minute.

A voice of authority said, "Who's this?"

"Mr. Gallo?"

"Who are you?"

"You and I should have a little talk."

"About what?"

"Your girlfriend."

"You son of a bitch."

"If I were a son of a bitch, I'd be calling you at home. I'm calling you at work so as not to make trouble."

"Listen, I don't know who you are or what your game is, but you picked the wrong guy. You make trouble for me, you're making trouble for yourself. That is not a smart thing to do."

"I'm not making trouble. I'm trying to help you."

"You got a funny way of doing it."

"You got girl trouble. I could help you out with that."

"I don't have girl trouble."

"That's not what your wife thinks."

"What?"

"Didn't she tell you? How Miss Hotpants

rang your doorbell and she chased her away."

"Are you kidding me?"

"She didn't tell you, did she? That's kind of creepy. If she called you on the carpet, demanded to know what was going on, that's one thing. But sitting on it, keeping quiet, gotta start you thinking. What's her game?"

"When was this?"

"Yesterday afternoon."

"How do you know?"

"Wanna have a little talk?"

"We're talking now."

"Not on the phone."

"Why not?"

"I don't trust your line."

"About a family matter?"

"How do I know that's all it is?"

"You called me."

"So?"

"What's your angle?"

"Not on the phone."

There was a silence on the line. The guy was clearly not used to people standing up to him.

"All right. Where are you?"

I told him.

"Okay, there's diner five miles south on the left hand side, just past the mall. Be there in fifteen minutes."

I stuck the cell phone back in my pocket and pulled out. Wondered if I was heading into a trap. A diner was where *The Sopranos* ended, the last we ever saw of Tony Soprano and his clan. Not to say that they died there, what with the ambiguity of the ending. Still, if I walked in the door and the jukebox was playing "Don't Stop Believing", I was going to freak out.

I drove south, keeping my eye on the odometer and wondering just how many diners there happened to be on the left side of the road. Not to worry. The shiny aluminum tube with the neon Diner sign had to be it.

I got out and glanced around the parking lot for any henchmen, gunmen, snipers, marksmen, saboteurs, cronies, hitmen, or thugs. I didn't see any, but that didn't mean they weren't there.

I also didn't see the man I was supposed to meet. Of course, I didn't know what he looked like. One small flaw in the plan. But not a real problem.

I walked in the front door of the diner, struck a pose, and glanced purposefully around. I figured I didn't have to know him, he'd spot me. I figured right. A man in a booth halfway down the row stood up, cocked an inquiring eye in my direction.

I walked over, said, "Mr. Gallo?"

"Yeah."

I extended my hand. "Mr. Smith."

I don't know if he believed it or not, but he sat back down.

I slid into the booth across from him. "You want to talk here?"

"I want coffee."

"And you waited for me? How nice."

"Don't be an asshole." He waved the waitress over, said, "Coffee."

"Two," I said.

He was a burly man in a suit and tie with a full head of curly, black hair, despite seeming close to fifty. His face, rounded but hard, seemed vaguely familiar. Like someone I recognized from the newspapers or TV, most likely a story on some indictment or investigation.

"All right," he said. "What's this all about?"

"A girl with the body of a porn star came to see you last night."

"The hell she did."

"Your son answered the door. She asked for you, but he came back with your wife. She offered to use the girl's body parts for origami."

"What girl?"

"Her name's Angela Russo. Vinnie Carbone's girlfriend."

His eyes flicked.

And the penny dropped.

I knew where I'd seen him before.

Going into the motel room next to the one I was staking out.

I tried not to betray my recognition and said calmly, "Mean anything to you?"

"What?"

"The girl's name."

"Can't say as it does."

"How about her boyfriend?"

He measured his answer. "I knew him. Not well, but I knew who he was. He did odd jobs for people. Sometimes he did them for me."

"In the 'salvage' business?"

He looked at me sharply. "What's that supposed to mean?"

"I looked for your company. I couldn't find it."

"You probably got it wrong."

"Yeah, that's probably it. So you don't know Jersey Girl?"

"Who?"

"Sorry. Angela Russo. Vinnie's girlfriend. You know, Vinnie, the guy who sometimes worked for you."

"I don't like your attitude. You're here

because you said you had something you didn't want to spill in front of my wife. That sounded bad, but it turns out it isn't. You don't know dick."

"You were meeting a girl at a motel."

His eyes flicked again. "Says who?"

"It doesn't matter."

He stared at me. "What?"

"It doesn't matter who's making these charges. What matters is whether they're making them to your wife. I'm not, so I'm your friend. But other people might. So, why don't you and I cooperate and see that doesn't happen."

"That sounds very much like a threat."

"If you listen, you'll see it's just the opposite. I mean, come on, think about it. If that were a threat, I'd be asking for money. I'm not asking for money. I don't want money. I may be able to help you. But it's hard, with you thinking everyone's out to get you."

The waitress returned, slid coffee in front of us.

I dumped milk in mine, stirred it around.

He'd banged two packets of sugar against his hand, tore off the ends, dumped it in.

We stirred our coffee, sized each other up.

"What's your angle?" he said.

I was afraid he'd ask me that. I didn't have

one. At least not one I could tell him.

"I'm sweet on the girl."

"What?"

"That's my angle. I like the girl."

"You're too old for her."

"I thought you didn't know her."

"I don't know her. I'm going by what you said. Body like a porn star."

I shrugged. "There's old porn stars."

He looked at me sideways. "You're kind of weird."

"You don't know the half of it. I like this girl. I don't want her to get hurt. Someone hurt her boyfriend. I'm hoping it wasn't you."

"That's silly."

"Not at all. Her boyfriend gets killed and she comes to your house. Rings your doorbell, pisses off your wife. Hard to believe she just came to cry on your shoulder. More like why'd you kill my guy?" I stuck a finger in his face. "Unless you were having an affair with her. Unless *she* was the girl you were meeting at the motel."

He scowled. "How many times do I have to tell you. I wasn't meeting any girl at any motel."

"Then what were you doing there?"

"What?"

"What were you doing at the motel if you

203

weren't meeting a girl?"

"Wait a minute, wait a minute. What are you talking about? I wasn't at any motel."

"Ever?"

"Huh?"

"I didn't say when this was. You haven't been to a motel recently, say within the last month?"

"Why should I remember that?"

"How hard can it be? You live in a nice house, why should you go to a motel unless you were shacking up. Which I would expect you to remember."

Tony thought that over. "All right, asshole. You made your pitch. I got nothing to say. You wanna talk to my wife, talk to my wife." He pointed his finger in my face. "But it will not be conducive to your health. You know what I mean?"

"I get the gist."

"Don't get smart with me. You stay away from my wife, if you know what's good for you. You got that?"

"Absolutely."

33

The woman who answered the door had curly hair and perky breasts, a far cry from the battle-ax who attempted to rip Jersey Girl's tits off on the front lawn the night before. She wore a lime-green pullover and a pair of sweatpants that might have been for running, but primarily served to emphasize a spectacularly rounded derriere. That may sound sexist, but I'm a detective and I'm trained to notice such things.

"Mrs. Gallo?"

"Yes."

I flashed my ID in the way I do when I'm hoping no one will actually look at it. "I need to ask you a few questions."

"About what?"

"Mind if we go inside?"

"Why?"

"I'd prefer to do this quietly, but if you'd like to come with me, that's fine."

She thought that over, blinked, stepped

aside. "Come in."

I followed her into the perfectly ordinary kitchen of a perfectly ordinary house. I don't know what I expected. Guns and drugs and hitmen, perhaps.

She stood at the kitchen counter, stuck out her chin. It almost cleared the tips of her breasts. "What's this all about?"

"I'm investigating a charge of aggravated assault."

"My husband isn't home."

"No, ma'am. And your son's not home either?"

"No."

"There's no one else in the house?"

Her eyes narrowed and she took a step back. "Don't get any ideas."

I sighed in exasperation at the aging process. What was acceptable once now just made me a dirty old man. I sat down to make her feel less vulnerable. "Sorry, ma'am. I don't mean to upset you. But these things come up. Do you deny being involved in an aggravated assault against Angela Russo?"

Her mouth fell open. "What are you talking about?"

"Yesterday afternoon. Right here, on your front lawn. Did you assault one Angela Russo?"

"I don't believe this."

I nodded. "Yes, ma'am. That would be your first reaction. But these things have to be investigated. I understand you had a dispute with the woman in question."

"No dispute. The slut banged on the door, asked to see my husband. I told her to get the hell off the lawn."

"And what is her relationship to your husband?"

"She has none."

"Then why was she here?"

"I have no idea."

I grimaced. "See, that's where your story falls apart. If the woman has no relationship with your husband and you don't know her from Adam, why would you go nuts when she knocks on the door?"

"I did not go nuts."

"Did you let her see your husband?"

"Of course not. What right does she have to see my husband?"

"I don't know. But when a stranger knocks on your door, the usual reaction is not to drive them away. At least, not without finding out why they're there. Did you ask her what she wanted with your husband?"

She smiled, leaned forward, inviting cleavage appreciation. "You're making a big deal out of nothing. The woman looked like she stepped out of a men's magazine. Who the hell did she think she was, banging on my door asking to see my husband? That's not how it's done. You want to see someone, you call first."

"You drove this woman away for a breach of etiquette?"

"I didn't drive her away. I told her she couldn't see my husband."

"Did you ask her why she was there?"

"I didn't care why she was there."

"Did you know who she was?"

"No."

"You didn't know her boyfriend had been recently killed?"

"No. How would I know that?"

"Apparently, he worked for your husband."

She said nothing.

"Did you know that?"

"How could I know that if I didn't know him?"

"Actually, if you don't know who her boyfriend was, it's very possible."

She blinked. "Huh?"

"If you don't know who her boyfriend was, how do you know he wasn't someone who worked for your husband?"

"You said he got killed. If someone who worked for my husband got killed, I'd know about it."

"And you didn't?"

"No."

"The name Vinnie Carbone means nothing to you?"

"No, it doesn't."

"As far as you know, this woman had no connection to your husband? She just rang the front doorbell and asked for him out of the blue?"

"We've been through all this."

"I'd like to pin it down."

"Wait a minute, wait a minute. You said 'aggravated assault.' Am I charged with anything?"

"No."

"Am I under arrest?"

"No, you're not."

"Then I don't have to talk to you. I've been very cooperative. I've told you everything you needed to know. I think we're done."

She stood up to indicate we were done.

I figured I'd done the best I could.

I left.

34

Calling on Jersey Girl again wasn't the best idea in the world, but I was running out of ideas. I'd already heard the aggrieved wife's side of the story, or lack of it, not to mention that of the oblivious mafia husband. It seemed like I should hear the story from the point of view of the other woman.

Besides, she already thought I was a cop, so I wouldn't have to go into any preliminaries. Which was probably the wrong way to phrase it when dealing with a woman who drops her robe at the slightest provocation.

Nonetheless, I pulled up in front of the house, knocked on the door.

She was dressed this time. I didn't know whether to count this as a plus or a minus, but she had on spandex pants and a leotard top. It did not appear as if she had wasted time putting on a bra.

She scowled when she saw me. "Why are you here again?"

"I have a few more questions."

"Yeah, well I wish you guys would get your act together. It's not enough dealing with the other cops, I gotta have you twice?"

I wasn't sure if her anger was that I was back or that I had resisted her charms. "Just a few questions."

"Right, it's always just a few questions. What did you find out about the gun? Silly question. If there was anything to it I'd be in jail."

She sat me down in the kitchen and said, "Would you hurry up, I have to get to work."

"There's this other matter. I understand you called on Tony Gallo."

Her mouth dropped open. "That bitch called the cops?"

"You are referring to Mrs. Gallo?"

"Of all the nerve. The woman attacks me and then reports me to the police."

"What did you want with Tony Gallo?"

"My boyfriend was murdered. I wanted to see if he knew anything about it."

"Why would he?"

"Vinnie worked for him."

"That's the only reason?"

"What other reason could there be?"

"You tell me."

"My boyfriend's been killed. No one knows why. The cops aren't doing a damn thing about it — no offense."

"None taken. So you thought Tony might have something to do with Vinnie's death?"

"No, of course not. I thought he might *know* something. In case it was work related."

"Now we're coming to it. What kind of work was your boyfriend doing that someone might want to kill him?"

"I have no idea."

"That's less than helpful."

"Well, excuse me. I didn't ask you to come here, ask stupid questions. You don't like the answers, that's too bad."

"Uh huh. You having an affair with Tony Gallo?"

"Who told you that?"

"Is it true?"

"Of course it's not true."

"Then why would someone tell me that?"

"I have no idea. I'm not responsible for what people say. I can't help it if someone gets the wrong idea."

"How would someone get the wrong idea?"

"I don't know. I don't think anyone did."

"His wife sure did."

"That bitch!"

"I gather you don't like her much."

"Are you kidding? She tried to kill me."

"You can swear out a complaint against her."

"Against Tony Gallo's wife? Oh, that's a great idea. How do you think he'd feel about that?"

"I thought you didn't know him."

"I know *about* him. Vinnie told me stories."

"Like what?"

"Nothing I'd repeat."

I grimaced, shook my head. "That's a bad attitude. See, that's *implying* that you're withholding evidence and conspiring to conceal a crime. You can go to jail for that."

She looked shocked. I could practically see her melt into seductive mode. If she'd been wearing a kimono it would have been on the floor. She put her hands on my arms, said, "Forget I said that. Can you forget I said that? It's got nothing to do with this. You were talking about Vinnie. And Tony's wife." Her eyes widened. "Say. Do you think there's something there?"

No, I didn't think there was something there. I thought she'd pulled the idea out of thin air in an attempt to distract me and make me forget about compounding a felony and conspiring to conceal a crime. Which I was perfectly willing to do, since I wasn't a cop, and even if I was, anything

213

Vinnie told her was hearsay and there was nothing illegal about withholding it.

I pretended to take the bait. "You think Vinnie might have been involved with Tony's wife? He ever talk about her?"

I could see her calculating her answer, trying to figure out how much trouble she'd get in making something up.

"He thought she was too young for Tony."

"Really? How'd that come up?"

"I don't know. Just making conversation."

"She's not that young. She's got a teenage son."

"Right."

"Vinnie say anything else?"

"I don't remember."

"What about Tony Gallo."

"What about him?"

"What did Vinnie say about him?"

She bit her lip.

"Well?"

"I'm trying to remember."

"Take your time."

"He said he was a bad man to cross."

"Really?"

She pounced on it eagerly. "Yes. So if Vinnie crossed him . . ." She smiled, spread her arms like what more did I need?

"How could Vinnie cross him? What was his job?"

"He never said."

"But you think it wasn't work related. You think Vinnie might have been involved with Tony's wife."

"It's possible."

"Ever accuse him of it?"

"Huh?"

"Ever ask him if he was sleeping with the boss's wife?"

"Of course not."

"Why of course not?"

"Never crossed my mind."

"But it does now."

"Now he's dead."

"Did it ever occur to you Vinnie might have something on the side?"

"No, it didn't."

"How about you?"

"Huh?"

"You have something on the side."

"That's rather personal."

"Yes, it is. Your boyfriend's dead. If you were involved with another man that might be the reason why."

"He killed Vinnie so he could have me all to himself?"

"Why is that so stupid?"

"It just is."

"You don't watch a lot of noir movies."

"What?"

"*Double Indemnity. Blood Simple. Body Heat.*"

"Was that with Kathleen Turner?"

The phone rang. She made a face, walked over, picked it up. "Hello? . . . Hi . . . Now? . . . Not a good time . . . I don't know, why don't I call you?" She hung up the phone, said, "Is this going take much longer? I gotta get to work."

"I think we're about done. I just wish you could give me a better reason for going to Tony Gallo's house."

"Vinnie's dead. I need to know why." She put her hands on my shoulders, looked up into my eyes. "Please. Find out why."

35

I staked out her house. I figured it was stupid. I knew she was going to work. But I had to do something. Because everything was circular, and nothing made sense. Here's a girl who leads me to Tony, who leads me to his wife, who leads me back to her again. What did all that mean?

The simplest explanation was, she and Tony Gallo were having an affair. Supporting that argument was the fact that Tony Gallo's wife had not acted kindly to the sight of her. She had exhibited every symptom of a woman whose husband was stepping out on her. It was so obvious it had to be true. The way I saw it, no other explanation was possible.

Which made me uneasy. Not that I don't trust my own judgment, but in the course of my less-than-illustrious career, I have found life kicks me in the teeth more often than not. The sure thing doesn't come in, the safe assumption isn't safe at all, and the hopelessly convoluted, barely possible long-shot is the explanation all along.

But, Jesus Christ, how much evidence did I need? The woman had the gun that killed her boyfriend. The boyfriend worked for the man who was presumably her lover. I presumed it, Tony's wife presumed it, any man in the North American continent who had a pulse would presume it.

The only fly in the ointment, the only rain on my parade, the only satisfactory, solution-spoiling cliché was, why in the name of reason would Jersey Girl's boy-friend be renting a motel room for his girlfriend and his boss? If Jersey Girl's boyfriend was indeed so accommodating and agreeable to an open relationship, why would they have to kill him?

And why would he have rented them a motel room next to a dead Aflac salesman?

I had to admit there were still a few kinks in my reasoning, but I put that down to re-ality kicking me in the teeth. If there weren't kinks in my reasoning, that's when I should get worried.

But that was the broader picture, which of course I didn't understand. But in the smaller scheme of things, examining Vin-nie's murder as a self-contained unit, it fit perfectly well. And it wasn't just because it was a noir movie plot. It just made sense that it was just what it looked like. And no matter how much I tended to doubt it, I could not stop myself from believing that the phone call Jersey Girl got was from Tony Gallo, and any moment now he was going to come driving up, park his car, and throw himself into her arms. Which couldn't happen in any case, because she was on her way to work and didn't have time.

So what I was actually doing was your basic rule-out: I was watching the house to rule out the possibility that Tony would show up after I left. Then I would have missed that valuable piece of information. On the minus side of the ledger was that it was a futile gesture. On the plus side of the ledger was that she was going to work, so it wouldn't be long.

I wondered just how long that might be.

It was five minutes.

Only she didn't go to work.

Tony Gallo drove up, parked his car, and went in.

He was out in twenty minutes. A suggestive time. Long enough for a quickie, and not so short as to necessarily categorize him as a premature ejaculator.

I, on the other hand, was coming in my pants. I mean, good lord, it shouldn't be such a big deal being right. But for me, having a sure thing come in was almost like having a long shot come in.

Tony Gallo got in his car and drove off. I let him go, immediately regretted the decision. I knew Jersey Girl was going to work. On the other hand, I only knew that because she told me so. And her word was not necessarily reliable on any of a number of subjects. If she was not going to work, doubtless it would not be the first fib the young lady had ever told.

She was out five minutes later. I checked her out for signs of disarray. I couldn't see any, but then Jersey Girl lived in a permanent state of disarray, so I'm not sure what I would have noticed. Anyway, she seemed to be wearing the clothes she'd been wearing before, and they were more or less on her body. Her scoop-neck did tend to scoop a bit, though that was nothing new.

Anyway, she hopped in the car and took off.

I followed, on the off-chance I would learn something.

I didn't.

Jersey Girl drove straight to the beauty parlor, went inside and went to work.

I hung it up and went home. Having let Tony Gallo go, there was nothing much I could do. I needed to evaluate what I'd learned, see how it fit in the general scheme of things. The only question was whether I should evaluate it in the presence of my attorney, who would not be pleased to learn how I had come by the information, or my wife, who would ridicule my theories out of existence. I opted for Alice, largely because I didn't happen to owe her twenty-five thousand dollars.

There was a traffic jam on the bridge, backed up all the way to where the roads divide, and blinking signs offer you a choice of the upper or lower lever with estimated waiting times for each. At the moment it was forty minutes for the upper, forty-five for the lower. I opted for the lower, even though it was a longer wait, because there are no exits off the approach to the upper. There are exits for Ft. Lee off the lower. These exits are marked, Exit Only — No Reentry To Bridge.

Ignoring the warning, I exited and drove a block alongside the highway, crossed Lemoine Avenue, and hung a left onto, you guessed it, the George Washington Bridge. It was the upper level, but that didn't matter. From there it was only a *two-minute* wait to the tollbooth. And it was only that long because some moron was blocking the E-ZPass lane, and I had to wait for him to move.

I went through the toll booth and proceeded slowly but steadily. Tie-ups on the way into Manhattan are largely caused by tie-ups on the Cross Bronx Expressway, which the bridge feeds into, and that seemed to be the case today. Not to worry. Coming off the bridge I took a right, curled around a squiggle of off ramps to the West Side Highway, where there was practically no traffic at all. I went south to Ninety-Fifth Street, got off, and took Riverside Drive back to 104th.

There was a parking spot on my block.

Some days you get lucky. I parked the car, folded in the driver's side mirror, zapped the doors locked. I went in, took the elevator up to my apartment.

The cops were there.

37

There were a bunch of them. Some in uniform, and some in plain clothes. The cops in uniform were New York City cops. The plainclothes cops might have been from anywhere, but two of them I knew. Bad Cop and Morgan, taking their act on the road.

Sergeant Fuller grabbed me, whirled me around, slapped handcuffs on my wrists.

"What are you doing here?" I demanded. "Get out!"

"They're searching the apartment," Alice said indignantly. It seemed to upset her more than the fact I'd been arrested.

"What the hell?"

"They have a warrant. They're tearing the place apart."

I had to bite my lip to keep from saying, "What are they looking for?" I knew damn well what they were looking for.

"Where's your car parked?" Fuller demanded.

"On the block."

He held out his hand. "Your car keys." When I didn't immediately produce them, he added, "I have a warrant to search your car."

"Oh, for Christ's sake."

"I also have a warrant for your arrest."

"What's the charge?"

"Obstruction of justice."

"Oh, for goodness sakes. That's one of those things that sound so lofty but actually means you don't know."

"And impersonating a police officer. Is that specific enough for you?"

Oh.

I'd been wondering how bad it was.

It was bad.

"I want to call my lawyer."

"I called him," Alice said. "He's on his way."

"Tell him to meet you in New Jersey," Bad Cop said. "You're going back."

"The hell I am."

"The hell you're not. I got a warrant."

"In New Jersey?"

"That's right."

"This is New York. Your warrant's no good here."

"You can argue that when your attorney shows up. Right now you're going to Jersey."

"The hell I am. I'm not waiving extradition."

Fuller frowned. "Extradition?"

"I wanna stay in New York. You wanna take me to New Jersey, you'll have to extradite me."

Fuller scowled at me murderously. I think his next move was to beat me unconscious and drive me to New Jersey strapped to the hood of his car.

Richard arrived just then. He took in the situation at a glance, struck a pose, and said, "What the hell is going on here?"

Bad Cop stuck out his chin. "Your client's under arrest. He was just explaining to us why he won't waive extradition."

Richard rolled his eyes. "God save me! All right, look. I don't know why you're discussing law with my client when you should be discussing it with me."

"Discussing? Who's discussing? I put the handcuffs on, he said, 'You can't extradite me.' Does that sound like a discussion?"

"He left a few things out," I said.

Richard put up his hands. "Boys, boys. I'm sure you both have legitimate complaints. The thing to remember is, I don't care. This is not a case of who gets sent to the principal's office. Let's see if we can walk the situation back a bit. Effect a compromise."

Fuller stared at him. "No one's compromising on anything. Your client's under arrest."

"I'm sure he is," Richard said. "Now, you wouldn't know it, but I actually have a law practice. In the interest of speeding things along, why don't you let me talk to my client?"

They did. Richard and I went in the living room and closed the door leaving the cops to cool their heels in the foyer.

"Okay, what's up?"

I gave Richard a rundown of the situation.

"Is that all they told you?"

"What?"

"That it's obstruction of justice?"

"And impersonating a police officer."

"Oh, yeah. That's no problem. We can beat that charge."

"Why?"

"Because you actually did it. Makes it easier to defend."

"Richard, I'm not finding this amusing."

"I wasn't joking. Impersonating an officer is a piece of cake. It's specific, we can prove you didn't do it. Obstruction of justice is so vague, it's damn near impossible to defend." He looked at his watch. "I wonder if it's been long enough."

"Long enough for what?'

"For them to think you're telling me what you did. I would hate for them to think I already knew all about it."

"What about extradition?"

"We are waiving extradition."

"Why?"

"Well, for one thing, they'll hold you in jail while you fight it. If you really want to stall on that basis it's a strange choice." He looked at me. "You saw that in some movie?"

"What?"

"Extradition."

"I read it in a book."

"Same difference. The main reason we waive it is we can't win."

"Why not?"

"The grounds for fighting extradition are extremely limited."

"How about the fact I didn't do it?"

"Oh, nobody cares about that. That's a matter to be decided in a court of law after extradition. As far as extradition itself is concerned, you're guilty until proven innocent."

"That can't be true."

"It is. Unless you establish a legal precedent. How'd you like to be quoted in court all the time, 'In People vs. Hastings, it was decided. . . .' " He looked at his watch. "It's been enough time. Let's go see how bad it is."

38

It was pretty bad. The way Richard pieced it together, the local cops, with no leads in the Vinnie Carbone case, made another pass at Jersey Girl, who, predictably said something to the effect of, "Oh, no, not again," and told them all about the nice detective who had interviewed her and taken possession of her gun. Which set off a chain reaction of accusations, protestations, and recriminations in various branches of the constabulary, until someone in the loop made the connection to the police officer who wanted photographs of the fatal bullet for a Ft. Lee cop involved in an entirely different investigation. Sergeant Fuller had not taken kindly to the suggestion that this detective represented him.

I don't know how long it had taken to straighten it all out, but somewhere in the course of all that, Sergeant Fuller had driven down to the Jersey Shore, confronted the officers at the precinct as well as the technicians at the lab, and browbeaten them into admitting that aside from the detective himself they had no evidence whatsoever that the person they had spoken to knew him from Adam.

Anyway, since I'd been arrested and booked, he had my mug sheet, complete with mug shot, which the cops and technicians unanimously identified as the culprit. For all Richard could ascertain, Jersey Girl hadn't seen it yet, but you could be sure she would.

Richard cocked his head at me. "Do you recall me suggesting that attempting to obtain a photograph of the fatal bullet would be an inadvisable course of action?"

"I think we can concede I fucked up, Richard. The question is what we're going to do about it."

"There's no point my doing anything about it if you're just going to do it again."

"Fine. I promise not to obtain any more photographs of the fatal bullet."

"I don't think you understand the seriousness of the situation."

"I do. I understand it without you beating it into me."

"If you did we wouldn't be here. You're like a compulsive gambler. You're in so far over your head you keep plunging on long shots and getting deeper and deeper in debt. The problem is, you're gambling with your life."

"They have the death penalty in New Jersey?"

"Gallows humor. The last refuge of a drowning man."

"Could you just skip the character analysis and concentrate on the situation?"

"The situation is bad. The situation would be bad even if I didn't have twenty-five thousand bucks riding on it. Talk about long shots. We're at a point now where there's no chance of making this go away. We're talking about how to beat it in court. And I don't mean in front of a judge. I'm talking about selling a jury. *Swaying* a jury is the long shot now. I'm talking about winning one juror and getting the jury hung."

"Yes, yes," I said impatiently. "You do a great job of painting a gloomy picture."

"Oh, really?" Richard said. "Because I'm just beginning. Right now you're charged with impersonating an officer and obstruction of justice. In addition to the murder charge you're out on bail for that I'm sure we can beat."

"I'm glad to hear it."

"But look what's happening now. The

cops are going nuts looking for a gun. Which you broke half a dozen laws to get your hands on. That's mighty suspicious. If I were a cop, that's the kind of behavior which would be apt to tip me off."

"Come on, Richard, can't we just concede that you're a wizard at sarcasm and this situation gives you boundless opportunities, and move on?"

"I thought I was. I guess the problem is your actions in this case are so stupid that simply reciting them smacks of ridicule. Here's the point. You scammed a woman out of a gun for no conceivable reason. So the cops are looking for one. The only thing that makes the least bit of sense is that the gun in some way implicates you."

My mouth fell open. "You're kidding."

Richard shrugged. "Do the math. You go to extraordinary lengths to get hold of the gun. You go to extraordinary lengths to get the photograph of the fatal bullet. Why in the world would you do that? The only conceivable reason is that the gun incriminated you."

"That's absurd."

"I know that, and you know that. But for all the cops know, it's true. The bottom line, in case you fail to grasp it is, they're trying to peg you for the second murder."

"Jesus Christ."

"What?"

"That's so stupid."

"Why?"

"Why would I kill Vinnie Carbone?"

"You have the hots for his girlfriend."

"Oh, come on."

"Wasn't she ripping her clothes off and prancing around naked in front of you?"

"They don't know that."

"They do if she tells them."

"Why would she tell them that?"

"Why not? You think a girl who would do it wouldn't tell it? This is not some shrinking violet. What if she says, 'I offered to fuck him and he'd still rather have the gun'?"

"Why would I turn her down if I've got the hots for her?"

"You must have really wanted that gun."

"Like I couldn't have had both?"

"So? What if you're some gallant principled hero type who wouldn't take advantage of her in her sorry state?"

"And yet I killed her boyfriend."

"These are good arguments." Richard shook his head. "I hope I don't wind up having to advance them."

39

We got the same judge. I suppose in a county that size it was inevitable; still it couldn't be good.

It wasn't. As the prosecutor droned through charge after charge, none of which, I was pleased to note, happened to include murder, the judge's face grew longer and longer. After a while it was like I was being arraigned by Seabiscuit.

The judge turned to Richard Rosenberg. "How does the defendant plead?"

"Not guilty on all charges. We would request reasonable bail."

The prosecutor nearly gagged. "Bail? Your Honor, we ask that bail be revoked and the defendant remanded to custody."

"On what grounds?" Richard inquired calmly.

"Is he kidding me?" the prosecutor said. "The defendant, as you know, is currently on bail for murder. While on bail, he seized the opportunity to meddle in a police investigation by impersonating an officer and obtaining evidence to which he has no right."

"Nonsense," Richard said. "Do you claim he was meddling in the case for which he was charged?"

"No. In another case entirely."

"Then I fail to see what one thing has to do with the other. Frankly, I resent the prosecutor attempting to prejudice Your Honor in this case."

"Oh, I doubt if that will happen," the judge said dryly. "But that is certainly not the type of behavior one would expect from a defendant out on bail."

"What behavior? I hope Your Honor is not deciding the case before it is tried. An accusation is not a conviction. My client is presumed innocent until proven guilty."

"How can you claim there is no connection when the arresting officer in the murder case is the officer he claimed to be representing?"

"Your Honor, are we arguing the merits of the case now? I thought this was a bail hearing."

"It's an arraignment," the judge corrected. "Your assumption of a bail hearing is optimistic."

"For good reason, Your Honor. The charges are much less serious than the ones for which he was previously on bail."

"Exactly," the prosecutor said. "The defendant is charged with a capital crime. And yet he persists in breaking the law."

"He does nothing of the kind. Which I will demonstrate as soon as the matter goes to trial. Unfortunately, this is neither the time nor place for such a presentation. This is merely an arraignment. The time for entering a plea and fixing bail."

"The defendant has forfeited bail."

Richard grimaced. "Oh. Forfeit. What a nasty word. Particularly when we're talking about my money. I would like to point out, Your Honor, that you set bail, I posted bail, and the defendant is out on bail. All strictly according to Hoyle. And there is no reason to alter that."

"He broke the law."

"That's your opinion. But you can't expect us to act on it."

"I beg your pardon. What do you think an arraignment is?"

"Gentlemen, gentlemen," the judge said. "If we could stop this petty bickering."

"Exactly," Richard said. "We can argue these things in court. Right now I'd like to set bail."

"Or rescind it," the prosecutor said dryly.

"Thank you," Richard said. "Rescind is a much nicer word than forfeit. Totally inaccurate, but much politer. Your Honor, would you please instruct the prosecutor that bail is not punitive. It is merely to make sure the defendant appears in court." He smiled. "Here he is."

"Hardly of his own volition."

"Really? I wish the prosecutor would make up his mind. Is it now his position that the defendant did nothing to precipitate his arrest? Was he picked up merely on a whim?"

The judge banged the gavel. "That will do."

"If I may answer that, Your Honor," the prosecutor said, "the defendant was picked up on allegation and belief that he had in his possession a gun purported to have been used in another crime. That is the evidence he falsely obtained by impersonating a police officer."

"And did he in fact have this weapon?"

"Search warrants duly obtained for his apartment, his office, and his car failed to produce it. I would ask the court to direct him to do so."

Richard put up both hands. "Whoa! The prosecutor is making wild allegations and assuming facts not in evidence. Is my client presumed guilty just because he says so? Is it not more likely to assume that if the police could not find a weapon it is because there was no weapon to find?"

"Are you claiming you don't have the gun?" the judge said.

"I'm claiming this is not the way to ask for it. The prosecutor can't say, 'I think you stole something, please hand it over so I can try you for stealing it.' "

"That is not the situation at all," the prosecutor said angrily. "I have a host of witnesses attesting to the fact that he has the gun."

"Then let them testify. But at the proper time. I thought this was merely an arraignment, but if you want to argue probable cause, let's go. I would love to get these charges dismissed right here and now."

They went on like that for some time, with the end result that I was arraigned on a whole host of chicken-shit charges, a probable cause hearing was scheduled, and the defense was served with a *subpoena duces tecum,* ordering us to bring the gun into court.

Aside from that, my bail was continued, and I was free to go.

40

"What are you doing here?" MacAullif growled.

"We gotta talk this out."

"You have a lawyer."

"I can't talk to my lawyer."

"Talk to your wife."

"I can't talk to my wife."

"I'm the lesser of three evils."

"Least."

"Huh?"

"You're the least."

"You may be wrong about that. I understand you got arrested again."

"You heard about that?"

"How could I not? Sergeant Fuller is the laughing stock of the police department. Sergeant Fuller does not like being the laughing stock of the police department. Sergeant Fuller is going to do everything in his power to see you go down."

"Yeah, but he was anyway. It's no big deal."

MacAullif's expression changed. "Oh dear. You've lost it haven't you? You've gone off the deep end. You've got yourself in so much trouble your brain can't process it. You escape to some rich fantasy land where you're the cocky PI, tossing off one-liners in the face of danger, aping some actor you saw in the movies. Who came out okay because it was a movie, and he was the star, and they didn't want to kill him off in case there was a sequel. You, on the other hand, are expendable."

"No one's gonna kill me off."

"Oh, no? You're playing footsy with mobsters and pissing off cops. Mobsters could rub you out. Cops could rub you out and make it look like mobsters rubbed you out."

"Oh, come on."

"I could rub you out just for coming here. You're living poison in the police department. I could get blackballed just for being seen with you."

"Do cops really say 'blackballed'?"

MacAullif slammed his fist down on the desk. "Stop it! I got a very short fuse on this one. You got something to say, say it and get out of here."

Victory. He was going to let me talk. As

241

opposed to picking me up by the scruff of the neck and hurling me out in the street.

"Okay. You know why the cops picked me up?"

"I heard the charges."

"Screw the charges. I mean how'd they get onto me? It's a separate county. It's a separate crime."

"Didn't you represent yourself as working for Fuller?"

"I may have said something to that effect."

"Don't be cute."

"Yes, I did. But there was no reason for anyone to check on it."

"No? The cops couldn't call up and say any luck with the bullet?"

"I suppose they could. Only I wasn't dealing with the cops in charge of the investigation. There were several degrees of separation."

"The guys from the lab couldn't call up and say any luck with the bullet?"

"Why would they? They're technicians. They supply data. They don't coordinate it."

"They couldn't be curious?"

"You're grasping at straws, MacAullif. Yes, some unlikely chain of events could have happened. But I'm not leaving it to chance. I'm saying is there a natural order of events that would make this happen?"

"Is there?"

"You're not nearly as much help as I hoped."

"All right, maybe your friend the forensic expert ratted you out."

"He claims he didn't."

"You asked him?"

"I asked if anyone had shown any interest in my findings. He said no."

"You believe him?"

"Seemed like an honest man."

"With your track record, he's probably peddling Uzis on the side. So what's your theory?"

"I'd rather hear yours."

"Yeah, but I don't have one. I'm sure you do."

"It's not really a theory."

"Of course not. It's a confused jumble of facts and surmises. Nonetheless, you believe it. You're here for validation. You don't care what I think. You just wanna sell me on what you think."

"I think there's a hidden connection. I think all these things are intertwined like some crazy ball of yarn. You keep picking up the ends and pulling them out, eventually you'll get one long piece of string."

"Really? A piece of string has two ends.

How many ends are you picking at?"

"That's the problem. Way too many. But we have connections. These crimes intersect at the motel. Vinnie Carbone rents a room. The guy next door gets killed. Vinnie Carbone gets killed. The cops haven't connected these two murders."

"They've connected them now. You've forced the connection on them. With your dumb-ass snooping."

"They may not make the connection. They may just see it as coincidence."

"How can they see it as coincidence when you rub it in their face?"

"You're right. I'm dumb for teaching the cops their business. We've been through this. Let's move on. All right, the point is, the connection exists, and we don't know what it is. But I know someone from Vinnie Carbone's room killed the Aflac salesman. I know that because I was watching the door and no one entered his room. And I know Tony Gallo was in the room Vinnie Carbone rented. I also know Vinnie Carbone worked for Tony Gallo and Tony Gallo had the hots for Vinnie Carbone's girlfriend. I also know Vinnie Carbone's girlfriend wound up with the gun that killed him. The cops don't know all that."

"No. They know *you* wound up with the

244

gun that killed him. Which you have refused to surrender."

"I haven't refused to surrender anything. I have been asked to produce evidence I do not have. Therefore I have not produced it. The police have searched my apartment, my office, and my car, and have not found it. But let's not harp on what I did. Let's examine the evidence. The gun that killed Vinnie Carbone is not the same gun that killed the Aflac salesman. We know that because the cops *have* the gun that killed the Aflac salesman."

"Right," MacAullif said. "There were two guns. As far as the cops are concerned, you were caught with both of them."

"Let's look at what the principles did," I said. "Someone gave the gun to Jersey Girl."

"She claims it was Vinnie."

"Yeah, but we know it wasn't, because Vinnie was shot with it."

"It could be true if she shot him."

"And held onto the gun? Still, leaving the gun that killed her boyfriend in her trunk is not that swiftest of all possible moves."

"Then how do *you* account for the gun?" MacAullif said.

"What if her boyfriend gave it to her?"

"You just got through saying he didn't."

"Her *other* boyfriend. Tony Gallo."

"Oh, wonderful," MacAullif said. "The guy's so hot for her bod, he kills her boyfriend, then gives her the murder weapon, so if things go bad she can take the fall. This guy is really a prince."

"Mobsters are not necessarily the best of role models."

"So, say you just shot your girlfriend's lover. What would you do with the gun? Throw it in the drink? Or give it to her to hold?"

"Well, we don't know all the facts."

"No kidding. All you got is theories, and they don't hold water. I haven't even heard a theory for this. Why does her lover give her the gun?"

"I don't know."

"So how does she wind up with it? If you don't have a theory for that, none of your theories hold water. The whole thing comes crashing down like a house of cards."

"You're mixing metaphors again."

"Damn it, will you take this seriously?"

"I'm taking this seriously. I can't tell you things I don't know. So far all I've got are questions. I'm trying to find answers that make sense."

"Questions like what?"

"Why does the Aflac salesman wind up dead?"

"He was mixed up in the mob."

"Why does his wife hire me?"

"Oh, what a straight line."

"I thought you didn't want to fool around."

"I don't want *you* to fool around. But if you're going to lob them across the middle of the plate."

"The wife hires me because she thinks he's stepping out on her. Does that make any sense? Yes, it does. If he's mixed up in the mob, and that's what he's hiding from her, and she naturally thinks it's a woman."

"So she hires you and he immediately checks into a motel and gets killed. Now, why does he do that?"

"He's following instructions."

"Check in and get killed?"

"Of course not. He's sent to a meeting of some sort. Perhaps he knows he's meeting Tony Gallo. Perhaps not. At any rate, Tony Gallo's there and kills him."

"You don't think he was meeting Tony Gallo?"

"Maybe he was meeting Vinnie Carbone. Tony Gallo was an added starter."

"And how does he wind up in that motel room?" MacAullif said.

"What do you mean?"

"Motel room number seven."

"He's told to ask for it."

"So Vinnie Carbone checked in first?"

"That's right."

"To a motel room with a connecting door."

"Sure," I said. "Otherwise it doesn't work."

I tried to control my excitement. I had turned the tables on MacAullif. He was questioning me, instead of me questioning him. Which meant he was leading the conversation, establishing theories through the Socratic method.

Of course, he was asking questions for which I didn't have the answers.

"How does Vinnie Carbone get a room with a connecting door?"

"He asks for it."

"He asks for a connecting door, but doesn't ask for the room that connects to it? Isn't that a little weird?"

"It may be weird, but it happened."

MacAullif made a face. "No, it didn't. Just because you say he must have asked for it doesn't mean he asked for it. There's no 'must' about it. He could have got it a number of different ways, and probably did. Because if he asked for it that would be a red flag in a murder investigation. You ask for the room next to the guy who got killed?

Not a good position to put oneself in."

"Well, how else could he do it?"

"He could ask for the room without asking for the connecting door. It's the connecting door that's the red flag, not the room. He says, 'Let me have unit eight.' "

"How does he know there's no one in unit eight?"

"There's no car in front of unit eight. This is not the type of place you check in and go out somewhere. This is a place for sleeping and fucking."

"Fine," I said. "So there's no car in front of unit eight, so he checks in, says, 'Give me unit eight.' How does he know there's a connecting door?"

"Can't you tell from outside?"

"How could you tell from outside?"

"The way the rooms are set up. Where the windows are. I don't know, something that makes the rooms different."

"I was watching that motel. For hours. Believe me, there was nothing different about the rooms."

"And you are the most observant PI on God's green earth."

"You saw the motel. Did anything strike you as different?"

"I wasn't looking for anything."

"Neither was I. But I'll bet you a hundred

bucks there wasn't. If we drive over there you'll see that's the case."

"We're not driving over there. I'll concede the point. At least for the sake of argument. There's no way to tell from outside whether or not there's a connecting door."

"So how did he know?"

"He must have stayed there before."

"Exactly," I said. "And that could be traced."

MacAullif's eyes widened in alarm. "Oh, no you don't."

"Relax, MacAullif. I'm not asking you to do it."

"And you're not doing it either."

"No kidding. The guy knows me as the killer. He knows you as the cop."

"He used to know me as the cop. By now he knows me as the guy impersonating a cop."

"You are a cop."

"Don't start that again. I'm not going back to that motel. I don't care if it was on fire and my wife was inside."

"Having trouble with your wife?"

"Fuck you. The point is I'm not going to do it."

"I know."

"And you *can't* do it."

I sighed. "No, I can't."

41

"What's my motivation?" Alice said.

"Huh?"

"Isn't that what you actors say, when you're pretending to take it seriously: 'What's my motivation?' "

"Your motivation is not to get caught."

"I know that part. I'm talking about the role I'm playing."

"You're playing the part of an unmarried woman checking into a motel."

"Unmarried?"

"At least not married to the man you're checking in with."

"How do you play a woman checking into a motel with a man who's not her husband?"

"Memory of emotion. You think back to the last time you checked into a motel with a man who wasn't your husband."

"Oh."

"Is that a problem?"

"Well, there's been so many. I can't remember which one was last."

"Never mind. Just try to act like we're not married."

"How do people who aren't married act?"

"Well, for one thing, they don't have any luggage."

"We *don't* have any luggage."

"Atta girl."

We were driving over the George Washington Bridge. Alice was joking bravely in the face of danger, what with me on the hook for two murders and all, but I could tell she was scared. One false step and this could blow up in our faces.

I pulled the car into the motel, stopped opposite the manager's office. Heaved a sigh of relief. It had sounded like a different guy on the phone, but I couldn't be sure. But the young man in the t-shirt and the baseball cap wasn't him.

"So, what's the plan?" Alice said. "You want me to distract the kid with my feminine wiles?"

"Save your feminine wiles until we get in the room."

"We're going in the room?"

"If you want to do method acting, you gotta carry it through. We're checking into a motel for an illicit affair."

"I thought it was to get you off the hook

for two murder counts."

"That's not what we're *playing.* We're *playing* illicit lovers."

"What's your plan?"

"You'll see when we get in the room."

"Stanley."

"We check in, scout out the office. Actually, *you* check in."

"Why?"

"So I don't have to sign the register Stanley Hastings."

"Couldn't you check in as John Smith?"

"He's already here."

We went into the motel office.

Alice batted her eyes, said, "We need a room. Do you have something quiet?"

I swear the young man suppressed a smile. "Yes, ma'am, we do. I can give you unit twelve. It's away from the highway." He looked like he was going to add, "And prying eyes," but he didn't.

"That will be fine," Alice said.

She paid with a credit card, signed the register.

We went out and got in the car.

"So?" I said.

Alice looked at me. "You saw it yourself."

"What do you mean?"

"Yes, you sign the register in a ledger book."

"Yeah. So?"

"Ledger's for show, computer's for dough."

"You sure?"

Alice gave me a look. "There's nothing in the register but signatures. When you leave, you'll get a computer printout of the charges. It doesn't matter what name you checked in under, it's billed to your credit card."

"What if you paid cash?"

"Then it will be listed as paid cash. Which would look mighty suspicious."

"So?"

"Let me at that computer."

We pulled up in front of our unit and got out.

"Where's the key?"

Alice handed it over. It was piece of plastic the size of a credit card.

"Excellent," I said. "This key doesn't work."

"That's a rather defeatist attitude."

I slipped the key into the slot in the door, pulled it out. A green light flashed. I pushed on the door while pretending to turn the knob.

"See?" I said. "The door won't open. Which is really bad news, because you have to pee."

"Right," Alice said.

We walked quickly back to the motel office.

"The key doesn't work," I told the manager.

"Huh?"

"We can't get the door open. And my wife really has to go to the bathroom."

"I really do," Alice said, shifting from one foot to the other.

For my money, Alice could have won an Academy Award for Best Performance of a Woman Who Has to Pee. And I was no slouch in the Man Unused to Calling a Woman His Wife or Referring to Her Bathroom Functions category.

The kid, for his part, managed a dopey grin. "Yes, Ma'am. Sorry about that. I'll give you another key."

"The key's fine," I said. "It's the door that won't open."

"What do you mean, the key's fine?"

"When you slide the key in and pull it out the green light flashes. But the knob won't turn. If the red light flashed, it would be the key. But when the green light flashes, it's gotta be the door."

"Don't argue with him," Alice said. "If he wants to give you another key, let him give you another key."

"It's not going to do any good if it isn't going to work."

"It's gonna work," the kid said.

"Oh, my God, I can't wait!" Alice said. "Don't you have a bathroom?"

"Right through there."

Alice rushed in, slammed the door.

"Let's get the unit open," I said.

"I'll make another key."

"I can hear you through the door," Alice said. "Are you just going to stand there and listen?"

"Come on," I said. "Let me show you the problem."

He hesitated a moment, said, "Yeah."

We went outside and down the row to unit twelve. It was nice he'd given us one at the end of the row. I tried to take my time getting there, but it wasn't easy. There was really no topic of conversation one could strike up under the circumstances. I considered faking a stroke, but that would just send him back to the office to call for help.

"Here you go," I said.

I dipped the card in the slot, waited till the green light flashed, pushed on the knob.

"Oh, for goodness sakes. Here, let me show you."

The kid took the card away from me, put it in the slot, pulled it out, watched the green light, twisted the doorknob and pushed the door open.

"See? You don't just push. You gotta twist the doorknob."

"Hey, let me try that," I said.

I took the card from him.

"Knock yourself out," the kid said.

He turned to go back.

"Hey, wait a minute," I said. "You go back there alone, you'll piss her off. Better you stay with me."

"I'm not supposed to leave the office."

"So? You *left* the office. Big deal. Let me try the card."

I dipped it in the slot, the green light came on. I twisted the doorknob counter-clockwise, pushed.

"Now it doesn't work."

"You twisted it wrong."

"Huh?"

"Twist it the other way."

"The other way?"

By now the kid must have concluded that if I got laid at all it would be a real miracle.

"Twist it this way," he said, turning his wrist.

"Oh. I see."

I did it right this time. The door opened.

"Okay. We're all set."

I couldn't think of another way to stall

257

him on our way back to the office. Tying my shoelace wasn't going to work. The guy would just keep going. And bringing him down with a football tackle might have roused his suspicions. I walked along beside him, prayed for Alice to be quick.

As we neared the office I raised my voice. "I feel really stupid about this. Thanks for being a good sport."

"No problem," he said, but he didn't break stride.

He went up the single step, flung open the office door.

"Oh, my god!"

"What's the matter?" I cried.

I crowded in behind him.

Alice was sprawled out on the floor in front of the bathroom door.

"I fell," she said. She struggled to her hands and knees. "I'm all right, I just fell."

"What happened?"

Alice glared at me. "I tripped coming out the door. Do you have to make such a big deal out of it?"

"I just want to make sure you're all right."

"I'm all right, I'm all right."

Alice twisted from my grasp, went out the office door.

I muttered a hasty thanks and followed.

I caught up with her halfway down the

row. "What happened?"

"I was trapped at the computer. I couldn't get back to the bathroom without being seen so I dived on the floor."

"Good move. Did you find the files?"

"I didn't have time."

"Damn it. I tried to stall."

"It's okay. I got this."

Alice opened her hand. Inside was a little gismo smaller than the door key.

"What's that?"

"A chip. I downloaded the files onto it."

"You got the files?"

"Yeah."

"Will they play on our computer?"

"Sure. Let's go home and take a look."

I shook my head. "We can't."

"Huh?"

"The manager already thinks something's funny. If we don't use the room, he's going to get suspicious."

Her eyes widened. "Oh, come on now."

"Sorry. We gotta stay at least twenty minutes. Gotta use the unit, gotta muss up the sheets." I smiled. "Think of it as method acting."

42

"Got it," Alice said.

"Already?"

We were no longer in the motel room. That was all right. We'd been there long enough. And God was in his heaven and all was right with the world. Which, coming from an atheist, should give you some idea of my state of mind. For once, I could take exception to Mick Jagger's assertion that you can't get no satisfaction, while agreeing wholeheartedly with his assertion that if you try some time you get what you need.

At any rate, Alice was hunched over her computer, typing furiously on screens no one outside of the geek squad knew existed, and it appeared that her labors had born fruit.

"What have we got?" I said.

"Reservations on file for the last three years."

"Three years?"

"Yeah. Apparently before that they weren't using the system. Either that or they stored the files."

"Three years should be fine. Do you have last week's reservations?"

"Sure do. Your client's husband, the guy you killed, registered in unit seven. Vinnie Carbone, the other guy you killed, registered in unit eight."

"That's nice. Can you tell if he ever rented a unit before?"

"Sure thing." Alice opened the window of a search engine I wouldn't have known was there. "I have nine matches."

"Dating back how far?"

"They're in the order of most recent. I'll have to skip to the end of the document, search in reverse."

"Never mind. What's the most recent?"

"About a week ago. Make that ten days."

"Same unit?"

"Yeah."

"Who's in the adjoining one? Or doesn't it show that?"

"Sure. I just scroll up. The program doesn't excerpt and list the entries, it just goes to them." Alice scrolled up. "Harold Deerfield. He used his credit card. He's from western Pennsylvania. You want the address?"

"Can I get it later?"

"Sure. I'll teach you how to use the program. It's easy."

I doubted that. The last time Alice taught me how to use a program, I not only couldn't learn it, but we nearly wound up in divorce court. Still, I wasn't going to waste time with the address of someone from western Pennsylvania.

"What have you got before that?"

"That would go back about two months. Same room, different guy next door."

Alice whizzed through the rest of the list. The entries went back about two years. As far as I knew there was nothing of any significance.

Alice reached the last one, read off the date.

Pulled up the unit next door.

Read off the name.

My mouth fell open.

Jersey Girl.

43

I had to see her. Don't get the wrong idea. I wasn't obsessed with the girl, no matter how enticingly her attributes might be displayed. But the case was all dovetailing together in a way I didn't like.

Here's a girl who stayed in the room with the murdered man. Granted, a few years earlier, but still. At the time, she had been next door to the other murdered man, who was her boyfriend, but wasn't at the time she stayed in the motel, though he was there.

I grimaced. Everything Jersey Girl touches seems to die. Discuss.

That was unfair. She hadn't touched my client's husband, at least not that I knew of. And staying in the same motel room two years apart barely qualified as an assignation.

Besides, I was still alive. Though she hadn't really touched me. Though not for lack of trying.

She opened the door in a sheer, something-or-other that just cried out to be backlit. I could imagine pizza delivery boys fighting for the assignment.

"You're not a cop," she said, accusingly.

Astute of her to notice. Though I'm sure it was pointed out to her. In fact, drilled into her head. "The guy you gave the gun to is not a cop, he's a murder suspect who probably killed your boyfriend."

"Who told you that?"

"A cop."

"He's probably lying. What if I told you *he* wasn't a cop."

She crinkled up her nose. "Huh?"

"If someone's trying to sell you a bill of goods, how do you know whether it's him or me?"

"He's a cop. He came with the cops."

"How do you know *they're* cops?"

"That's stupid. You're just trying to confuse me."

Yes, I was. But I wanted to get in the door. And it wasn't just the diaphanous negligee Jersey Girl was wearing. Though I had to admit she had perky nipples in it.

"You really want to talk in the door? You're hardly dressed."

"I don't want to talk in the door. I wanna

close the door."

I knew she did. Which is why I had my foot in it. The old traveling salesman's trick. I blamed myself for thinking *traveling* salesman. All door-to-door salesmen stuck their foot in the door. Traveling salesmen were the butt of numerous jokes, all of which involved a nubile young daughter. Which didn't really apply in this case, but, hell, Jersey Girl was *someone's* daughter.

The was no reason to shy away from physical contact. Aside from that touch-of-death thing. I squeezed by Jersey Girl into her house.

"Hey!"

"Sorry, but I don't have time to be polite. Some very stupid policemen think I'm mixed up in a murder."

"Yeah, right. You come around, say you're a cop. Take my gun. Lie about it. But, oh no, you're not mixed in anything."

"Did you tell the cops you gave me the gun?"

"What do you think?"

"With you, I don't know. You might have decided to deny having the gun."

She put her hands on her hips. "Well, that would be mighty stupid, wouldn't it? I thought I gave it to a cop."

"What happened to disillusion you?"

"Are you serious? They hauled me in. Asked me questions. Wouldn't let me go when they didn't like the answers."

"So you gave them answers they *did* like?"

"I told them the truth."

"Cops don't always like the truth. Sometimes you have to invent."

"I didn't lie."

"Good. Telling the truth takes far less brain power. You don't have to think so hard keeping your stories straight."

Jersey Girl went for her purse.

"You got another gun?"

"Huh?"

"I'd hate to get shot in your kitchen. It would be embarrassing as all hell."

"You're weird." She pulled a card out of her purse.

"What's that?"

"The cops said to call if you showed up."

"That's a poor thing to tell me. If I were a bad guy, I might try to stop you."

She drew back in alarm. "Is that a threat?"

"It's free advice, which is almost as bad." I flopped into a chair. "Go ahead and call if you want to. But think of what you're doing. You'll be calling the police, which is never a good idea under the best of circumstances, and these are not the best. If the cops connect you to the crime, you're dead."

"They don't connect me to the crime. They connect you to the crime."

"So you say. And they probably say so too. But do you always believe what you're told? The cops are going to tell you I'm the suspect whether they suspect me or you. Because they're not going to tell you *you're* the suspect. They're going to let you hang yourself."

"I'm not the suspect."

"You had the gun. You *claim* you gave it to me. Well, maybe that puts me in possession of the gun, but where did I get it? Think about it. What's more likely. Did you give me the gun *I* used to kill your boyfriend, or did you give me the gun *you* used to kill your boyfriend?"

"Huh?" She crinkled up her nose again. I wondered if it was real or just an affectation. I might have to watch *Jersey Shore,* see if they did it too.

"Keep with me here," I said. "Your boyfriend's dead. By your own admission, you had the gun. That's what the cops have now. If they get anything else that points to you, you're dead meat."

"What are you talking about? Nothing points to me."

"Ever stay at the Route 4 Motel?"

Her face drained of color. "What are you

talking about?"

"You don't know? Then why does it bother you so much?"

"It didn't bother me."

"Something sure did. I wouldn't expect even the Bates Motel to get a reaction like that."

She crinkled up her nose again. "What?"

"Good God, I'm too old."

"You're talking funny again."

"And you're changing the subject. I asked you if you ever stayed at the Route 4 Motel, and you went white as a sheet. I happen to know you stayed at the motel, but the cops don't know it yet. So, like I say, it would probably be a poor time to call them right now."

"I don't know what you're talking about," she said. But she walked away from the phone and sat down.

"I'm talking about coincidence, the law of averages, and dumb luck."

That got me a nose crinkle.

"Sorry, I don't mean to be enigmatic. Here's the deal. Your boyfriend got killed, you wound up with the gun. Not good, but you could probably explain it away. However, Philip Marston got killed in the Route 4 Motel, in the room you stayed in. Right next door to the room your boyfriend stayed in."

"What are you saying?"

"You know what I'm saying. When the cops connect you to the second murder, they're gonna have some more questions. And they're gonna be harder to answer than the first."

"What second murder?"

"Oh, come on, give me a break. Didn't you know Philip Marston?"

"Who?"

"You didn't know he was dead?"

"I didn't know he was alive. Who is he?"

"Damn."

"What?"

"I'm inclined to believe you. But tell me about your stay in the motel."

"I don't have to tell you anything. You're not the cops."

"No. But if you don't, the cops will get an anonymous tip, and they'll ask you a bunch of questions you'll *have* to answer."

"Fuck you. You've got a lot of fucking nerve."

"Two years ago you registered at the Route 4 Motel. Your boyfriend registered in an adjoining unit. With a connecting door."

"Oh."

I could see the wheels turning. Her eyes

got calculating, shrewd.

"And you want me to tell you about that?"

"It would pass the time."

"Huh?"

I sighed. "Sorry. I'm being facetious. I apologize. Tell me about the motel."

"You want to know about two years ago when Vinnie and I registered in separate rooms?"

"That's right."

"Why?"

"To see if it means anything."

Her nose went again. If I were her mother, I'd have warned her it might freeze in that position.

"Vinnie and I had just started dating. I wasn't going to stay in the same room."

"Why were you there at all?"

"Huh?"

"Vinnie has a house. You have a house. Why would you have to go to a motel?"

"He was married."

"Vinnie was married?"

"Well, maybe not married, but he was living with someone."

"Were you?"

"That's none of your business."

"Actually, it is. I'm trying to figure out why you had to go to a motel."

She thought that over. Once again, I could

see the wheels turning.

"I wasn't living with someone. But Vinnie was afraid his girlfriend would come by my house."

"She know about you?"

"She suspected."

"So you drove all the way up to Ft. Lee and went to a motel?"

"Yeah."

"And registered in separate units."

"Well, I didn't know him that well."

"So why was his girlfriend jealous?"

"Girlfriends are always jealous."

"Anyway, you stayed in separate rooms."

"That's right."

"Next time you only got one room."

"Huh?"

"The next time you stayed with Vinnie it was in one room."

"Well, I knew him better. First time it might not have worked out. Turned out it did."

"And then Vinnie got rid of his wife, or girlfriend, or whatever, and you became his girlfriend."

"Yeah."

"So you didn't have to go to the motel with him anymore."

"Yeah. So?"

"Vinnie kept registering at the motel. If it

wasn't with you, who was it?"

"You mean Vinnie was cheating on me? I don't believe it. That's a horrible thing to say."

"Maybe I'm mistaken. When was the last time you were at the motel?"

"The last time?"

She was repeating my questions. A typical stalling device of someone thinking up a lie. I wondered what lie she could be thinking up. It was a perfectly straightforward question. *When was the last time you and Vinnie stayed at the motel?* It didn't require a lie. Any answer would work. Why did she think it wouldn't?

"It's been a while," she said.

"Over a year?"

"Yeah."

"He's been there since then. You're saying it wasn't with you?"

She snapped her fingers. "Business!"

"Huh?"

"He sometimes rented a room for business. He must have rented the same room."

"Why would a guy like Vinnie need a motel room for business?"

"You forget who he worked for. He could have had business in that room."

"With Tony Gallo?"

"Sure. He worked for Tony Gallo."

"Why would he have to meet with Tony Gallo?"

"They could be meeting someone else."

"Philip Marston?"

"Who?"

She didn't know. I was sure of it. Though, as Alice points out, it would not be the first time I was wrong.

I was out in fifteen minutes, not sure if I was any wiser than before I came.

At least she hadn't called the cops.

44

I sat in the car and thought things over. No, not in front of her house. It would be just my luck to have a passing cop pick me up. The difference between a stalker and a detective on stakeout would be negligible. In either case I'd be screwed.

I was in the parking lot of a Route 4 mall. There was no shade anywhere in the lot, the sun was beating on the roof. I started the car, turned on the air conditioner, let it blast right in my face. Wondered how long it would be before a cop tapped on my windshield and told me I couldn't have the car idling.

Jersey Girl had cheerfully admitted staying with Vinnie Carbone in the motel. Her explanation of why they'd had two rooms and then one was pretty thin. So was the reason for Vinnie keeping the room after they stopped using it.

On the other hand, her assertion she and

Tony Gallo weren't having an affair also rang hollow. Was it conceivable Tony was making Vinnie rent a room for Tony to share with Vinnie's girlfriend? That seemed unusually cruel. But then, maybe Tony Gallo was one of these sadistic sons of bitches who got off on dominating others, making them bend to his will. Forcing his subordinates to perform odious tasks, the more shameful and degrading the better.

If that were the case, who killed Vinnie and why, and how did Jersey Girl wind up with the gun?

I had one solution I didn't particularly like. Vinnie Carbone, unable to stand up to his boss, stands up to his girlfriend and demands to know how *she* could treat him like that. He loses it, starts beating on her, and she has to shoot him.

I realized that premise actually had several outcomes. I had chosen that particular one in order to make a case for her self-defense. Which was really silly. She didn't deserve such consideration. If she were some hatchet-faced, flat-chested spinster, I'm sure self-defense would have never sprung to mind.

Which was pretty stupid. The girl shouldn't get a pass on her looks. Even if that scenario were true, it meant she was stupid enough to have hung onto the gun.

No matter. I didn't like the idea that she shot him at all. I mean, as a solution. I much preferred Tony Gallo shooting him. The motive was a little hard to find. The way I figured, if Tony was guilty, it had to be for another reason altogether. Tony would not kill off one of his henchmen in order to gain better access to his girlfriend, who was already making trouble for him with his wife. That just didn't add up. No, if Tony killed him, it was either because Vinnie pissed him off, or because Vinnie had become a liability.

The way I saw it, the main way Vinnie could be a liability would be to implicate Tony in the first murder. Tony had been there. Vinnie had rented the room. At the very least, Vinnie must have suspected what went on, even if he wasn't there. Which he wasn't, necessarily. If he could rent the room for Tony to have trysts with his girlfriend, he could rent the room for Tony to rub someone out. Though he didn't need to know he was renting it for that purpose.

If that was true, he might have been less than happy when he found out. Particularly when he realized his name was on the credit card receipt, and if the cops got pointed in the right direction, he'd be the one to take the fall. Vinnie might have protested being placed in that position.

Tony might have countered the complaint with a gun.

That seemed a lot better than the jealously angle.

If that was true, it meant Tony Gallo killed Vinnie Carbone and then gave the gun to Jersey Girl. Perhaps in the hope of killing two birds with one stone, if the girl had become a liability by making trouble for him with his wife.

Never mind that.

The point was, if Tony killed Vinnie to cover up the murder of the Aflac salesman, why did he have to do that? I'd been arrested and charged with the murder. No one suspected anyone else. Granted, I was out on bail, but that didn't mean the cops didn't think I did it.

So what set Tony off?

45

"What if it's cause and effect?"

MacAullif scowled. "Forget it."

I looked hurt. "Hey."

"Don't play innocent with me. That's one of your enigmatic opening statements designed to make me super-curious to know what you're getting at. I don't *care* what you're getting at. I got no patience with this one. You wanna talk, talk, otherwise get out of my office before I hit you with a chair."

"I'm going nuts trying to find a motive for Tony Gallo killing Vinnie Carbone, and I got too many. Tony was sweet on his girlfriend. Vinnie may have been sweet on Tony's wife."

"What?"

"I don't think he was, that's just a theory his girlfriend offered up, trying to find something that didn't implicate Tony or her. The other theory, and the one that makes more sense, is that he got rubbed out in conjunction with the hit on the Aflac sales-man. Only problem with that is it happens way after the fact, and he's peripheral as all hell. Unless it's cause and effect — and don't throw the chair, I'll tell you what I mean. Aflac salesman gets whacked, I get arrested, Richard gets me out. Since I didn't kill him and no one went into that room, we come up with the connecting door theory. You run a bluff on the motel man-ager, come up with the name Vinnie Car-bone. Vinnie Carbone is promptly whacked."

"You're saying the *motel manager* is mixed up in this?"

"Why not? The meetings were always at his motel."

"Meetings?"

"Vinnie Carbone kept renting the room. Long after he needed to share it with Jersey Girl."

"Wait a minute. Wait a minute. What are you talking about?"

"Two years ago Vinnie Carbone stayed in the same room. Jersey Girl stayed next door. Where the guy got whacked."

"And just how do you know that?"

"My wife may have peeked at their com-puter."

MacAullif rolled his eyes. "Unbelievable.

May have peeked at their computer. Do you have any idea how many violations of the penal code are contained in that one simple sentence?"

"Alice is a big girl. She can stay anywhere she wants."

"I thought we agreed you weren't going near the motel manager."

"He wasn't there."

"My god, do I have to close every loop-hole?"

"Water under the bridge, MacAullif. The point is, here's what we've got."

I gave MacAullif a rundown of the motel situation.

"Interesting," he said.

"Yeah. Jersey Girl tells an unconvincing story about staying there because Vinnie had a girlfriend, staying in two rooms because she didn't know him that well, and then one because she did. She categorically denies staying there with Tony Gallo. She can't imagine why Vinnie would have rented the room if it weren't for business."

"Oh, so this is *her* theory?"

"That doesn't make it wrong. Despite the fact that most of what she says is suspect. She's banging Tony Gallo. Tony Gallo's wife, incidentally, has a terrific temper and might be inclined to kill someone."

"Vinnie Carbone?"

"I have some theories there."

"I'm sure you do."

"One, she's pissed off at him for arranging the rendezvous between his girlfriend and her husband."

"Thin. If she was going to kill someone, she'd kill her."

"Sure, but Tony'd know she did it, even if the cops didn't. On the other hand, if she can kill Vinnie and make it look like his girlfriend did it, she's killed two birds with one stone."

"And how does she do that?"

"Plants the gun on her. Which I'm sure any New York cop worth his salt would have found, but their New Jersey counterparts don't."

"You said that, not me."

"Anyway, that's how I see it. The motel manager's in league with Tony Gallo. Which is why his motel is used for high-level meetings of the mob."

As if he could read my mind, MacAullif stuck a finger in my face. "You stay away from the motel manager."

"I won't go near him. But it would be easy enough to see if he has a record."

MacAullif threw up his hands. "Finally we come to it. You can't just talk things out.

You've always got an ulterior motive."

"I don't think it's ulterior, MacAullif. I think it's rather central."

MacAullif snatched up a vial from his desk, popped a pill in his mouth, swallowed it down.

"What's that?"

"Blood pressure medicine."

MacAullif must have been really trying. As I went out the door it occurred to me the whole time I was in his office he hadn't cursed once.

46

The motel manager was white as a sheet. "You stay away from me."

I put up my hand. "Hey, not to worry. You got nothing to fear from me. So you identified me. It was your civic duty, you had to do it. But don't worry, I'm not a threat." I paused, added, "Physically."

He blinked. "Huh?"

"If you were involved in the hit, you've got a lot to fear. Not from me, from the cops. Well, from me indirectly, because I'll turn you *in* to the cops. Right now I know more than they do. That's because they're sold on the idea I did it. I happen to know I didn't, which gives me a big edge. What's more, I happen to know the game you've been playing with Tony."

"Tony?"

"Don't play dumb. You know who I mean. Anyway, I'm putting the squeeze on your operation here. Not as payback for the murder rap — hell, those things happen. No, I'm doing it because it's my civic duty. Just like you ID'ing me. But it's not payback. Not at all."

"I don't know what you're talking about."

"Of course you don't. You just manage a motel. You got nothing to do with the mob."

"You're crazy. You get the hell out of here."

"I'm going. You just think about what I said."

That was my litmus test. I figured if he was connected with the mob, I'd hear from Tony Gallo. If he wasn't, the cops would pick me up.

The cops picked me up.

47

It was my old friends, Bad Cop and Gotsa-goo, or as I now knew, Sergeant Fuller and Morgan. You'd think they'd get tired of seeing me, but, oh no, every time I turn around, there they are again.

This time they nabbed me on the approach to the George Washington Bridge, cleared a lane with their sirens to let me get off. They hauled me out of my car, stuck me in the back of theirs.

"What is it this time?" I said.

Bad Cop had not mellowed toward me. "Guess."

"I haven't got a clue. I sure hope someone isn't dead."

Fuller's eyes narrowed. "What makes you think someone's dead?"

"I *don't* think someone's dead. I have no *reason* to think someone's dead. Except every time you pick me up, someone is. If that happens to be the case, do let me in on

285

it, because I'd like to know who I'm charged with killing this time."

"You think you're pretty smart, don't you?"

"No, I don't. And my wife can back me up on that. Is someone dead?"

"No one's dead. It appears you've been impersonating an officer again."

"Who says so?"

"Angela Russo."

"Who?"

"Vinnie Carbone's girlfriend."

"Oh, Jersey Girl. That's absolutely false."

"You deny you've been harassing her?"

"Her ass. Nice play on words. Did you mean that?"

"Do you deny you called on her again?"

"Called on her? Is that a crime? I thought you said impersonating an officer."

"Well, that's what you're charged with."

"Old news. I've already been arraigned. Or do you have something else?"

"You know what I mean. You've done it again."

"Done what again?"

"Impersonated an officer."

"I beg to differ. I've *never* impersonated an officer. And I've certainly never done it *again*."

"When's the last time you talked to Angela

Russo?"

"Gee. I'd have to consult my social calendar."

"Don't be an asshole. You want to be arrested again?"

"You mean I'm not?"

"We're just talking here. If it's a friendly talk, maybe you go on your way."

"That's nice. How'd you find me?"

"Huh?"

"You dragged me off the George Washington Bridge. How'd you know I was there?"

"We bugged your car."

My mouth fell open.

Bad Cop grinned. "Gotcha. Boy, that one always gets 'em."

"You didn't bug my car?"

"Sorry to disappoint you, but it's too much trouble getting the warrant."

"I don't think he appreciates your sense of humor," Morgan said.

"So how'd you know?"

Fuller ignored that question, said, "You find that gun?"

"I'm afraid I can't comment on the subject of a court subpoena."

"Of course not."

"And you guys know that. So why'd you pick me up?"

No one answered.

I looked at them, considered. "You had no reason to pick me up. And you have no right to hold me. Unless you bring me in and charge me with something."

Bad Cop shrugged. "We could do that."

"Go ahead."

They didn't. We stood there staring at each other, and nothing happened.

It was wonderful. I called their bluff and beat 'em. I nearly swaggered as I got out and walked back to my car. No one stopped me. I backed up and drove off.

I was feeling pretty good until I realized I was still on the hook for murder.

48

I was running out of options. I had tweaked the motel manager and it hadn't led to Tony Gallo. That didn't mean Tony Gallo was innocent, merely that the motel manager probably was. Not surprisingly, all my efforts had come to naught.

"You're doing fine," Alice said.

"Fine? I'm charged with murder."

"Aside from that."

"Are you trying to be funny?"

"No. But it's an absurd charge, and it's gonna go away. Meanwhile, you're making progress. You poked the motel manager and Tony Gallo didn't react."

"The cops did. That means he called them."

"Of course he did. You're a murder suspect he ID'd, and you're hassling him. Any rational person would call the cops."

"That means he's innocent."

"So?" Alice said.

"It would be easier if he was guilty."

"It would be easier if the killer confessed, said he was a bad boy, and promised not to do it again. Stanley, this is a good thing. Every time you eliminate one person from your list of suspects you wind up with a shorter list. You tweak the motel manager and he goes to the cops. You tweak the Jersey Shore bimbo and she *doesn't* go to the cops."

"She took her clothes off."

"Exactly. It's her first line of defense. With the motel manager it's the cops. With her it's her body. That makes you suspicious. Among other things."

"What other things?"

"Voyeuristic. Tumescent."

"You're enjoying this too much, Alice."

"I'm not enjoying this too much. It's a real conversation killer in almost any social situation. 'How's your husband doing?' 'He's being tried for murder.' You'd be surprised at how few people have a follow-up question."

"Alice. Do you suppose you could direct your razor-sharp wit toward getting me out of this predicament?"

"How could I do that? I don't have all the information. There are a number of questions here, and you don't have the answers.

Until you do, it's hard to know what happened."

Questions? Oh, dear. Was the Socratic method rearing its ugly head?

I took a breath. "All right, Alice. What questions would you like answered?"

Alice considered. "Why did the widow hire you?"

"Huh?"

"That's the first question, isn't it? That's how this all started. The woman hired you to follow her husband. Why?"

"He was cheating on her."

"Yeah, but he wasn't. He went to a motel. He'd didn't meet a woman, he got shot."

"He didn't know that."

"Why not?"

"Because it makes no sense. Would you go to a motel if you knew you were going to get shot?"

"It probably would not be my first choice of accommodations."

"You're having too much fun, Alice."

"I'm not having fun at all. I'm trying to make some sense out of the situation. You're the one saying things like, 'Would you go to a motel to get shot?' "

"Well, that's what you were implying."

"I was doing nothing of the sort. You're the one who suggested he went to a motel to get shot. That's absurd. He didn't go a motel to get shot. He didn't go to a motel to meet a woman. The truth lies somewhere between the two."

"You think he went to the motel to meet Tony Gallo?"

"Well, Tony Gallo was there, wasn't he? In the next room. With the connecting door. So he goes to the motel to meet Tony Gallo and Tony Gallo kills him."

"Why?"

"I don't know. But say he does."

"Okay, say he does. What's your point?"

"Why did the widow hire you?"

49

For a widow, she looked good. Which figured. She'd also looked good as a wife. Come to think of it, she'd looked good as a widow the last time I'd seen her. Basically, the woman just looked good.

She was surprised to see me. Which said something. After all, she had a doorman, he'd called upstairs, she knew it was me. And yet, she looked surprised.

She took me into the living room, sat me on the couch, just as if it were a social occasion. She was wearing a spandex something or other in lime green. I wondered how long her husband had to be dead to forgive the color.

"I don't mean to be rude, but why are you here?"

"You hired me."

She stared at me. "That employment is over."

"Why, yes, it is. But the consequences

aren't, and you're entitled to a report."

"A report?" The widow Marston could not have looked more surprised had I told her I was secretly Spiderman. "You've got to be kidding."

"No, I took the money, and I ought to give value, no matter how extenuating the circumstances. How much do you know about the second murder?"

"What second murder?"

"So you don't know. Let me bring you up to speed." I gave her an abbreviated version of the Vinnie Carbone killing. "The guy who had the motel unit next to your husband's was murdered. Vinnie worked for a mobster named Tony Gallo. Vinnie's girlfriend may have been involved. She's alleged to have been holding the fatal gun."

"Alleged? Why alleged?"

"The cops haven't been able to find it."

I figured that covered the situation.

As with Jersey Girl, I could see the widow's wheels turning.

"What's this got to do with me?"

"If it's related to the murder of your husband, it's got a lot to do with you."

"But it isn't related to the murder of my husband."

"No, because the private investigator you hired killed him on a whim."

She took a breath. "I don't know what your motive was. I don't know what you hoped to gain. I'm trying to forgive you. Well, maybe not forgive you, but I'm trying not to jump across the table and gouge your eyes out. Unless you've got something else you'd like to torture me with, could you have the decency to leave me alone?"

"Just tell me one thing."

"What?"

"Why did you hire me?"

"You know why I hired you. To see if my husband was having an affair."

"He wasn't."

"I didn't know that."

"What made you think he was having an affair?"

She opened her mouth, closed it again. "I don't have to answer your questions. I don't have to justify myself to you. The police think you killed my husband. You've given me no reason to think differently. I think this interview is over."

It was frustrating. Unless the woman seriously thought I killed her husband, you'd have thought she'd have been more interested in who possibly did. The problem, of course, was that I'd damned myself with my own story. According to me, I was the only one who went into that room.

I left the widow Marston's feeling more depressed than ever. Alice had challenged me to find out why the widow hired me. After my conversation with her, I was not one whit closer to knowing.

50

I staked out her apartment, which wasn't easy. In case you're thinking of becoming a PI, staking out an apartment in Manhattan is whole different ballgame than staking out a motel in New Jersey. It's not just peeing in a Gatorade bottle anymore. It's what are you going to do with your car? You can't sit in it because you can never get a parking spot close enough to the door. If you double park or sit by a fire plug, you're screwed, because if your quarry leaves on foot you can't leave your car.

Parking in a garage is suicide, in case the person you're tailing comes out the door and climbs into a car parked on the street. You can never get your car out of the garage in time, and you're left hailing a cab, which is bad news, because if the person took a car instead of a cab, they're probably leaving town, which means you either wind up with a 250-dollar cab ride, or with a cab driver who won't go.

The compromise I opted for was a meter on Madison. It had the disadvantage of having to be fed, and if I left the car and followed her on foot it would most likely run out. This particular spot had the advantage of being only two cars down from the corner. While I couldn't sit in it, it was easier putting quarters in when my hour ran out. I could go to the corner of Madison, look back down the block toward the widow's apartment building while I got my quarters ready. Then I could dash to the car, feed six quarters into the meter, and dash back, leaving the narrowest window of opportunity during which the widow might get away. Assuming she wasn't running, which well-dressed widows leaving apartment buildings seldom were, in the few seconds I was at the meter it was unlikely she would be able to exit the building, reach the corner of Fifth Avenue, and disappear from sight before I could see her. Granted, I am no track star; still I felt I could hold my own in the twenty-yard, six-quarter, widow-beating dash. (I cannot imagine why this has not become an immensely popular Olympic event — if the ratings for curling can go through the roof, surely anything's possible.)

Anyway, there I was, with my car on the meter and my eye on the door. I was watching from the Fifth Avenue corner, because it kept my options open. The street was one-way east, so if she headed toward Fifth she was going on foot. Unless she hailed a cab on Fifth, in which case I'd have to hail one too, and put up with the ticket, if not the towing charge, along with Alice's analysis of why I shouldn't have gotten it.

I had just fed my six quarters into the meter and sprinted back to the corner feeling mighty damn proud of myself, when a car came out of the underground garage. I had no idea what kind of car the good widow drove, so I didn't know if it was her, but whoever it was, they were coming my way. I shrunk back into the shadow of the buildings, watched the car for a clue.

I got one.

The car was a cream-colored Lexus sedan, just the type a wealthy widow might drive.

And the widow was driving it.

I turned my back, walked to the corner, and sprinted down Madison. I hopped into my car, gunned the motor, pulled out, and drove to the corner.

Damn.

The light on Madison was green, but I couldn't go through because I didn't know which way she was going. I drove up to the light and stopped. The cab behind me gave me the horn, the universal Hey-asshole-they-got-any-colors-you-like? treatment. I ignored him, switched on my blinkers. The cab pulled out and went by. The driver gave me the finger and cursed me out in a language befitting his turban.

I waited for the green light to change red. It did, letting the traffic on the side street go. The widow Marston was second car from the corner. I couldn't tell if she had her direction signal on — the car in front of her was obscuring the left headlight. The first car pulled out, revealing the truth. The left turn signal was indeed blinking. The widow was turning up Madison.

Only now I had a red light. Presumably, she'd get one at the next corner, unless she really gunned the motor and caught it just before it turned. The lights on Madison are staggered — the one on each block turns green slightly after the one on the previous block. Which meant they also turned red slightly after the one on the previous block. So, if you hung a left onto Madison the instant the light changed, and drove like a NASCAR driver, you could catch the light just as it was turning, not to mention every subsequent light.

I didn't think the widow was a NASCAR driver. On the other hand, I couldn't take the chance. As soon as she made the turn I ran the light, sending a delivery boy jumping out of the way. I sped down the block, thanking my lucky stars I hadn't gotten pulled over for a moving violation, and heaved a sigh of relief. The widow was waiting at the light.

She drove up Madison to Ninety-seventh Street, hung a left, and went through Central Park. She got on the West Side Highway, heading north.

It occurred to me that my surveillance would likely come to naught. On the other hand, where was she going? After all, she was recently widowed. Not that recently widowed people can't drive. Still, priorities change. Driving from necessity might still play. But joyriding would probably slip down the list.

I wondered if she was going upstate. Maybe she had a country house. I realized I knew nothing about the family. I should have looked her up. Though that didn't seem to be an issue, what with her husband getting killed. Of course, once I was pegged for the killer, it wouldn't have hurt to know a little more about them. But I hadn't suspected the wife, not until Alice asked me why she hired me. And I couldn't come up with a reason. Having a country house would indicate she had money. Money was always a motive for murder. Granted, not by an invisible assassin in a room full of mobsters, still if she had a country house in Mount Kisco, it would be nice to know.

She didn't.

At 181st Street, instead of getting left for the Saw Mill River Parkway, she stayed right for the Cross Bronx Expressway and the George Washington Bridge.

And a monumental traffic jam.

The West Side Highway north is always jammed at rush hour. And it's not the bridge. It's the damn Cross Bronx Expressway. Eastbound traffic is always backed up, and it impacts everything. Especially the northbound exit ramp from the West Side Highway. That's because the two-lane exit feeds both east and westbound traffic. And it's not like one lane goes to the expressway and the other to the bridge. The *two* lanes feed into *four* lanes, which would be all right, except the *inner* two lanes go to the expressway and the *outer* two go to the bridge. And since the expressway is always clogged, the two inner lanes back up into the two-lane approach ramp, which means the cars bound for New Jersey can't *reach* the two lanes bound for the bridge.

I sat in my car, waiting for the traffic to thin out and keeping my eye on the widow's Lexus one car length ahead. The saving grace was she couldn't go any faster than I could.

I had just had that thought when the widow reached the point where the ramp widened out. She pulled into the left-hand lane and headed for the bridge.

Good Lord.

She was going to Jersey. She was going to Jersey, which meant I just hit pay dirt, only I hadn't hit pay dirt, instead I'd blown the whole thing because I was a car length back, still in the bottleneck where I couldn't get out of line, and there she went around the approach ramp to the bridge.

The woman ahead of me was dawdling along. I gave her the horn, cruel and unusual I know, but I leaned on it hard.

She reacted instantly.

She slammed on the brakes.

I nearly ploughed into her. Instead, I received a number of angry glares from nearby motorists, already pissed off at being in this colossal backup, and not pleased to have someone interrupt the conversation they were having with their husbands, wives, or whoever on their cell phones, a no-no which could get them pulled over, except no cops could get near enough and there was no *over* to pull.

And there went the widow Marston, curling around the ramp and merging onto the George Washington Bridge, carrying with her all my hopes and fears, not to mention the solution to the case.

I stifled the urge to put the car in low and floor it, pushing right through the back of the woman's car. I contented myself with creeping up on her bumper and squeezing left, as if wishing could widen the gap. Miracle of miracles, her car moved.

I squeezed through the narrowest of opening, and rocketed onto the bridge.

51

This was it. This was pay dirt. Unexpected, but there had to be some connection. That had been the problem all along. What was the connection between a Manhattan Aflac salesman and a henchman from the mob? And there was the answer right in front of me all the time: Julie Marston. The guy's wife. My client. Who set the whole thing in motion, and set the whole thing up. This was what Alice's question had implied — and what a profound insight that was. *Why did she hire you?* She hired me to set me up. Or if not set me up, at least make me a witness. To be in a position to testify that no one went into that motel unit. Not that she expected to frame me for murder. That was serendipity on her part. She expected to be awakened by a call from the police telling her that her husband had been found dead in a New Jersey motel. Either that, or a call from me, telling her the police had just arrived and gone into her husband's motel room. As the wife, she'd be in a position to report to the police that I'd been on the job. In fact, if I were the one calling in, she'd probably instruct me to *go* to the police, identify myself, and demand to know what was going on.

In either case, there I would be, hung out to dry, telling a story that on the one hand made no sense, but on the other hand exonerated everyone, especially her, from the crime. Then I, like a dope, rush in and get caught with the gun. As far as the widow Marston is concerned, things couldn't be better. It's nice for her when I get arraigned, super annoying for her when I keep coming back.

It was a nice solution. Far-fetched and hard to prove, but it answered the two burning questions: Why did the widow Marston hire me? And what was the connection between Philip Marston and Tony Gallo? The connection was Marston's wife. Because Jersey Girl wasn't having an affair with Tony Gallo. Jersey Girl was a beard, the one he wanted the cops and his wife and everyone in the world to *believe* he was having an affair with.

I didn't know how it worked. I didn't know all the details. But as soon as it was confirmed, everything should fall nicely into place. All I needed was a connection. And here she was, driving over the George Washington Bridge. No way, no way did a recently widowed woman get dolled up, hop in her car, and drive through rush-hour traffic to New Jersey to go shopping at the mall. No, she was meeting Tony Gallo for dinner. Or to go to a motel. Surely not the *same* motel — the case was mind-blowing enough without that happening. Hell, with my luck they'd probably wind up in the same *room,* and what was left of my brains would come dribbling out my ears.

No, that wasn't going to happen. But she was meeting Tony Gallo, I was sure of it.

While I was thinking all that, she got off in Ft. Lee, drove straight to the police station, parked the car and went in.

52

Alice was infuriatingly supportive.

"It's not the end of the world."

"I'm glad to hear it. I thought it *was* the end of the world. Your revelation it's not certainly cheers me up."

She smiled. "Don't be cranky."

"Cranky? That's what you call it? Cranky? I apologize if just missing being cleared of a murder charge makes me a little testy."

"You sound like you got convicted. Nothing happened. You're just grousing because you didn't get the case dismissed."

"Aren't you upset? It was your theory. And it seemed so good."

"It wasn't a theory. I just asked why she hired you. It's a perfectly logical question. You're making too much of it because you see it as an attack on your competency."

"Competence."

"Huh?"

"You don't need a *y*. It's already a noun."

"You *are* upset. That's why you lash out with the grammar. Telling me I can't put a *y* on it. Are you sure about that? I've heard of competency."

"*Y* makes it an adjective. Like competency hearing."

"Right. That's how I get you declared incompetent and take all your money. Luckily, you don't have any."

"Ah, the silver lining," I said. "I know you're just trying to kid me out of it, but it isn't working. You may have to take your clothes off."

"It's not as bad as all that."

"I'm not saying it's bad. I'm just saying take your clothes off."

"Not right now."

I hate that phrase. Seemingly innocuous, but the moral equivalent of the twelfth of never or when hell freezes over.

"It's really not that bad," Alice persisted.

"How is it not that bad? Look what I've done. I tried to drive her into the arms of her lover and wrap up the case. Instead, I've driven her to report me to the cops. Any minute our doorbell's going to ring and they'll arrest me again."

"Then I guess I can't take off my clothes."

"Was that ever an option?"

"You're not concentrating. Look. You had

a theory, you tested it, it didn't work out."

"It was *your* theory."

"I'm not crushed. You seem to be, but, hey, that's the thing about theories. They're hypothetical until you test them. Some work out. Some don't. If they don't, you abandon them, or you devise another test."

"It's a little bit more than not working out. She went to the cops."

Alice waved it away. "Yes, yes, yes, yes, yes. That blows your fine-spun theory about how she was having an affair with this mobster out of the water. And you wonder why that doesn't upset me. It wasn't my theory to begin with. All I said was the woman must have had a reason for hiring you. That didn't have to be it. You took a button and sewed a vest on it."

"I always wondered about that expression. Are there people who sew buttons on vests?"

Alice ignored the deflection, pushed on. "Basically, it has to do with you undervaluing yourself. You don't trust your own opinion, so you put too much credence in other people's. An idea isn't necessarily right just because it's mine."

"Can I quote you on that the next time we have an argument?"

"You know what I mean."

I knew what she meant. The problem was,

she didn't mean it. She didn't think the idea was likely to be wrong just because it was hers. She thought it was likely to be wrong because of my *interpretation* of her idea. She still believed her idea was right. And would have been proven right, had I not carried the hypothesis through to its logical conclusion, but instead applied some circuitous logic no one in his right mind would have ever thought of, just to validate what she said. Which wasn't really to venture an opinion anyway, just to ask the question. Which, should the answer turn out to be enlightening, would prove her astute. On the other hand, should it not prove to be enlightening, she never said it would.

And yet, our marriage endures.

53

Richard wasn't thrilled when I dropped by to see him the next morning.

"You drove her to the cops?"

"I didn't drive her. She took her own car."

"Are you trying to be funny?"

"I'm trying to stay sane. This case has my head coming off."

"Why in the world would you call on the widow?"

"It seemed like a good idea at the time."

"Why? What could you possibly hope to gain?"

"I thought it might clear me of a murder rap."

"You don't trust me to get you off?"

"Of course, I do. Still, I'd rather not be cleared on a technicality."

"No, you'd rather be convicted. Which is what will happen, if you keep doing what you're doing."

"What do you think of my theory?"

Richard rolled his eyes. "Words can't describe what I think of your theory."

"What's wrong with it?"

"What do you think is more likely: husband got involved with mobster and got killed; or husband's *wife* got involved with mobster, who killed *him* so he could have *her*?"

"That doesn't have to be the motive."

"I'm glad to hear it. Usually, when you get some idea in your head, nothing can shake it. Are you telling me there's wiggle room?"

"The widow's involved. I don't know how, I don't know why, but she is."

"What makes you think so? Go ahead, make your case."

"Well, for one thing, why does she hire me?"

"This does not necessarily make her guilty. After all, *I* hired you."

"Not to tail a spouse who isn't cheating on you and subsequently winds up dead."

"Something the widow couldn't have foreseen."

"She could if she planned it."

"I see. It's a conspiracy theory, which is why you like it. You figure everyone's out to get you. Anything that supports that position must be true."

"I'm not having fun, Richard."

"Well, how much fun do you think I'm having? Here you are, getting into one scrape after another, and I'm the one who has to get you out of them."

"For which I'm grateful. But to get back to the premise. Woman hires me to catch her husband with another woman. He isn't with another woman, but he winds up dead."

"Kind of ironic, isn't it?"

"What do you mean?"

"If he was having an affair, he'd be alive."

"Right. And his wife would be suing him for divorce, and I'd have gotten paid, and everyone would be happy."

"Who'd she think he was having an affair with?"

"She didn't know."

"You say that with such inflection. As if you find it suspicious."

"Don't you?"

"Not suspicious enough to support your premise."

"Okay. You're the demon cross-examiner. Tell me why my premise is wrong."

"Oh, dear. How much time have we got?" Richard considered. "It would be easier to tell you what's right."

"Okay. What's right?"

314

"The way I see it, only one thing supports your story."

"What's that?"

"She went to the police."

I blinked. "That's the thing that *undermines* my story."

Richard smiled, in that maddeningly self-satisfied way he has when he thinks he's being clever. "She was one of the prime witnesses against you. As far as the cops are concerned, she's a rock star. You think she wouldn't have their card?"

"So?"

"So why does she go there? She's got their number. If she wants to report you, all she has to do is call."

"Maybe so, but the fact is she went."

"Yes, she did. And you have no idea why. So we move on. Where'd she go when she left the police station?"

My face fell.

"You don't know?"

"I didn't wait."

"Of course not. She went to the police station, confirming your own conspiracy theory. Why would anything else matter?"

"I just didn't think of it."

"You didn't think at all."

"Oh, yeah? How much grief would you have given me if I'd staked out a police station, particularly that one?"

"Oh. It's not that you didn't think of it, you thought I'd disapprove."

"I'm not saying I thought you'd disapprove, I'm just saying you would have."

"The point is you didn't think. Just as it didn't occur to you she could have called the police station. It wasn't a moot point. If you consider that she could have called the police station, the question is why didn't she? Why did she go there instead? The most logical answer is, she stopped in on her way somewhere else."

"I get the point."

"And yet you continue to offer justifications. Why can't you simply admit you fucked up and move on?"

"I'm trying to move on. You're the one who keeps harping on it."

"Fine," Richard said. "I will not bring up your idiotic behavior again. The point is, for whatever reason, tailing the widow didn't work."

"Yeah."

"So what you gonna do now?"

54

MacAullif seemed genuinely confused. "What do you think you're doing?"

"What do you mean?"

"Never mind that you're not getting anywhere. I can't even figure out where you're trying to get."

"I'm trying to find the connection."

"What connection?"

"Exactly. I'm trying to find *any* connection. There's two women in the case, Jersey Girl and the widow. I figure one of them's involved with Tony Gallo. I figure if I put a little pressure on her, she'll go there. I pressure Jersey Girl. The cops pick me up. So I figure it's the widow. I pressure the widow. She goes straight to the cops. Now I don't know what to think. If they're both clean, I'm nowhere."

"You think only good guys go to the cops?"

"I think killers are unlikely to appeal to

cops for help."

"What does Richard think of your theory?"

"Richard's got a theory of his own."

"Oh? What's that?"

I gave him Richard's the-police-station-must-be-on-her-way-to-somewhere-else-or-she-would-have-phoned theory.

MacAullif nodded approvingly. "For a negligence lawyer, the guy's got a clear mind."

"You have a low opinion of negligence lawyers."

"Doesn't everybody?" MacAullif considered the situation. "So, if I understand you correctly, you're trying to find out who's having an affair with Tony Gallo. You follow Jersey Girl to see if she goes there, but she doesn't, she turns you in to the cops. You follow the widow to see if she goes there, but she doesn't, *she* goes to the cops. Do you by any chance see the error of your ways?"

"What do you mean?"

"If you want to see who's having an affair with Tony Gallo, don't follow every girl in the world and see if she goes there. Follow Tony Gallo."

55

I staked out Tony Gallo's house at six thirty in the morning, which was a major pain in the ass, him living on the South Shore and all. I had to get up at five in the morning myself. I staggered around getting dressed, trying not to wake Alice or the dog. I might have succeeded if I hadn't stepped on her tail. The dog's. She barked and woke Alice. Then I had to explain what I was doing. I'd explained it the night before, but at five in the morning some details are not that easy to recall. My name, for instance. Alice called me a lot of things, none of them Stanley.

The dog was never going to let Alice go back to sleep, so I had to walk her before I left. The dog. I took her out to pee, which she did gratifyingly in the street, without making me go all the way to Riverside Drive. I took her back, threw her in the apartment, holding the elevator door open with my foot, went back down, got in my car, and drove to New Jersey to stake out a hood.

At six thirty the house was dark. The mobster was either there, or he, like I, had left without waking his wife. Much.

It was already light out, and I hated that, because it meant I could be seen. Sitting in the street in my car. For no discernable purpose. With New York plates.

I was very unhappy to be there, and I had to wonder if my initial decision to follow the women I suspected of being involved with Tony Gallo instead of Tony Gallo himself, stemmed from an extreme reluctance to follow Tony Gallo due to the fact that people who followed Tony Gallo might well wind up dead. I hadn't consciously had that thought before. At least I wasn't conscious of having consciously had that thought before. Which I guess amounts to the same thing. Anyway, I had that thought now. I kept expecting Clemenza to pop up in the backseat of my car, a la *The Godfather,* and slip a wire around my neck.

It occurred to me, that would solve my problems.

Time crawled. I sat there in my car, envisioning the worst. Which was easy to do. Things had to be pretty bad for MacAullif to advise me to follow Tony Gallo.

MacAullif's initial advice had been to stay a football field the fuck *away* from Tony Gallo. And here he was suggesting it, as if it were my last chance, a hail-Mary pass, an onside kick, a no-hope challenge flag thrown in desperation, oh how the hell did I get into football idiom, I really was losing it.

I tried to calm myself, focus my mind on something other than my imminent demise. I started recalling jokes from my schoolboy days. The elephant jokes, for instance. Remember them? The elephant jokes were of a similar theme, usually involving the gratification of the elephant, and ranging from the inane:

How do you get an elephant off the wall? You jerk him off.

To the poetic:

Jack and Jill
Went up the hill
Riding on an elephant
Jill got down to help
Jack off the elephant.

Or the Tom Swifties, in which everything Tom said came with a modifier:

"I'm really into homosexual necrophilia," said Tom, in dead Earnest.

Despite such diversions, time crawled.

321

By seven o'clock, the neighborhood started waking up. Lights were going on in some of the houses, including the one I was parked in front of. No, not Tony Gallo's. I wasn't parked in front of his house. I was across the street and a couple of houses down. I didn't expect that to fool a mob hit man; still I was taking every precaution.

Tony Gallo's house was still dark. That figured. It was summer, his teenaged son wouldn't have to get up for school. His wife looked like the late-rising type. And Tony, being his own boss, wouldn't worry about being late to work.

He was out the door at seven thirty.

Wouldn't you know it, I was peeing into my Gatorade bottle. Stupid, I know, but I wanted to get it out of the way, and there hadn't been a light in the house. Anyway, Tony Gallo comes out the front door and there I am with my dick in my hand. If you're a private eye, that's not the way you like to write it up in your report.

Tony cut across the front lawn and climbed into the back seat of his car.

The back seat?

Oh. My. God.

Did that mean what I thought it did?

What else could it mean?

Seconds later, the car roared to life and

pulled out of the driveway.

Sure enough, a young, greasy-looking thug was driving.

The guy was sitting in the driveway the whole time. He must have gotten there just ahead of me. I wondered if that was the daily routine. Have the car there by six thirty in case Tony wants to go. Or if the guy was assigned at six today, and Tony got held up.

I also wondered if this had been one of Vinnie Carbone's jobs.

I also wondered if I'd been spotted. I mean, the guy was sitting there parked in the driveway with the car facing out. How could he *not* see me? The guy would have to be blind. Or asleep. If you're waiting for a mob boss, do you *dare* fall asleep? Or would Tony just poke you in the shoulder when he got in the car and everything would be cool?

They came roaring by. I kept my head down. Not a fun prospect, with my dick out and a jar full of piss. Still, better than letting Tony get a look at me. The guy knew me. As what, I wasn't sure, but getting caught parked in his neighborhood couldn't be good.

I managed to zip my pants and get the top on the Gatorade bottle. I started the car, swung an inconspicuous-as-all-hell U-turn, and set off after the mob.

Tony Gallo's driver took enough loops to make me wonder if we were headed toward some deserted lot. Instead, he got on the New Jersey Turnpike heading north. That worked for me. It was the way I came. If nothing else, I was heading home.

Traffic was getting heavy, but we made good time and I had no trouble keeping up.

After about a half hour we reached the exit for the Lincoln Tunnel. It's an exit, but it's more like a fork in the road. The highway divides with huge signs stretched across the top offering a choice between the George Washington Bridge and the Lincoln Tunnel. We opted for the tunnel. I found that disappointing. The bridge is in Ft. Lee, along with the motel and the cops and the crime scene. Was it asking too much to expect Tony Gallo to return to the scene of the crime?

Only we didn't go in the tunnel either. We got off the turnpike and went in the opposite direction, away from New York. So. Tony had business somewhere else in New Jersey. That wasn't surprising. The man was connected, he could have interests all over. Whatever they were, they didn't concern me, unless they were women, and it was too early for him to be calling on a woman. At least I hoped it was. I mean, if these guys got laid first thing in the morning, life really wasn't fair. On the other hand, I wanted him to lead me to a woman, it just wasn't likely until the end of the day. In all probability I would follow him around all day in the course of his business, and if it were to include an amorous interlude it would be much later on. Which was a major pain in the ass. If the guy just had a normal business address like everybody else, I could have picked him up there at the end of work. But, no, he has to be a will-o'-the-wisp with a bogus address that you can't pin down and the cops can't pin down, so nobody can pin anything on him, and probably never would, even though he is most likely the perpetrator of any number of crimes, including those the police had reason to believe were mine.

I wondered what presumably illegal but probably incredibly boring business venture I would be treated to. More than likely I would wind up staked out in front of some storefront, trying to avoid the notice of Tony's driver, assuming he didn't get to go inside.

After a couple of miles we got off the highway and drove past a couple of refineries from which I could not discern a particular product, but could discern a particular smell. We followed smaller roads through what must have been incredibly undesirable real estate, boasting no factories, businesses, or private homes of any kind. I kept way back, and was a couple of hundred yards behind, when Tony's car turned off onto a side road.

I drove up on the turn carefully, fully prepared to go right on by in case the road was a dead end or in case Tony had pulled off and parked. But Tony's car was nowhere in sight. A dirt road led off into what appeared to be a desolate wasteland and disappeared around a bend behind an outcropping of rock.

What the hell?

I did not want to follow Tony Gallo down that road. But I sure wanted to know where he was going. Was this where he conducted business? Did he have some underground bunker?

I turned onto the dirt road, drove up to the bend, and stopped dead.

Tony Gallo's car was parked in what appeared to be an abandoned rock quarry.

Not good. If I could see him, he could see me.

I threw the car into reverse, backed up as

quickly as I could out of sight around the bend.

Should I turn around? I couldn't. I had to know what he was doing.

Which was probably nothing. He probably just stopped to take a piss. It wouldn't have been my first choice for a pit stop, but then a guy with a Gatorade bottle shouldn't cast stones.

So what are you going to do? The guy probably saw you, and any second he's going to come roaring out with guns a-blazing. There you'll be, stopped like a schmuck. Back up, turn around, get the hell out of there.

I got out of my car, scrambled up a mound of dirt to the outcropping of rock. Crawled to the edge, peered out.

They hadn't seen me. They had gotten out of the car, and were walking away toward the far end of the quarry. They were walking single file, with the driver ahead, and Tony walking slowly, purposely behind.

Good Lord. Was Tony going to whack his driver? That seemed a little harsh. Maybe he wasn't as good as Vinnie Carbone, but the guy had only been on the job a few days. Surely he deserved a second chance.

While I watched, they went around a bend I couldn't even tell was there, and disappeared from sight.

Moments later they were out again, heading for the car.

So what were they doing? What the hell was back there? Why the hell —

Heading for the car!

I crab-crawled back from the edge, pounded down the hill, leaped into my car, gunned the motor. Backed up, turned around, and drove off as quickly as I could without sounding like a pack of Hell's Angels.

At the paved road I turned right, figuring Tony would go back the way he came. I rocketed down the road, hung a U-turn, pulled off to the side out of sight.

Moments later Tony's car appeared. Sure enough, it took a left turn back the way he came. I gave him a head start, tailed along behind.

We went right back the way we'd come all the way to the Jersey Pike. We didn't get on it though, we went right on by. We appeared to be heading for the Lincoln Tunnel.

We were.

We went through the tunnel — no problem for me, I got E-ZPass. Richard gripes that he doesn't get individual receipts anymore, just a summary at the end of the month, but he doesn't sit in the long lines at the toll booths. Neither do I. I whiz through with E-ZPass, a convenience when calling on a client, a must when tailing a car.

We came out of the tunnel in midtown Manhattan, wove our way through the garment district, loading docks and delivery trucks on the side streets, office buildings on the avenues.

Tony's driver stopped in front of an office building on Seventh Avenue. Tony got out of the car and went in. I did not follow. Tony had a driver to wait in the car. I did not. Street signs were screaming, NO PARKING, NO STOPPING, NO STANDING. Tony's driver was stopping and standing. I guess he figured that didn't apply to him.

He figured right. When a cop banged on his window, the driver rolled it down, flashed some ID at him, and the cop went away, looking miffed at not being able to hassle someone.

He made up for it by hassling me. He tapped on my window, made me move. I had no magic ID to flash. I drove around the block, hoped like hell the car would be there when I got back.

It was, but so was the cop. He gave me the evil eye. It occurred to me Tony's driver wouldn't have an official ID. He was being accorded Driver-of-the-Mobster status. I wondered if I should make an issue of it.

I drove around the block again. Wondered if this happened to other PIs. *Yeah, I lost the guy I was tailing. Cop made me move my car.*

Third time's the charm. The car was there, the cop was gone. I pulled up to the curb just as Tony Gallo came out of the building with a young business type. Bit of a flashy dresser. It seemed to me there was something a little sharp and sleazy about him, but it could have just been because he was with Tony Gallo. Anyway, the guy had a shit-eating grin on his face, and he was talking to Tony in an ingratiating, toadying manner. Which, I got the feeling, was the way most people talked to Tony Gallo.

Tony opened the back door and the man got in. Tony got in beside him, and the car took off. That was a stroke of luck. The cop had just come around the corner.

I pulled out, took off after them. We looped around a few blocks, went into the Lincoln Tunnel.

I wondered if we were heading for Ft. Lee. That would be nice. Tony Gallo obviously did business in Ft. Lee, and aside from whacking people in motel rooms, I had no idea what it was. Just like everything else in this damn case. Come on, Tony. Throw me a crumb.

Only Tony didn't. On the other side of the Lincoln Tunnel he got off the highway. We were going in the opposite direction, so it took me a moment to realize it was the same exit as before. But passing the same used car lot removed any doubt.

I felt a hole in the pit of my stomach, like I'd swallowed an ice cube, and it was burning my insides. I know that sounds confused as hell, but at that moment, that's what I was. Because I suddenly realized this guy was being taken for a ride!

That had to be it. Tony, ever cautious, scouted out the place, then picked up the guy for the hit. That's why the guy was grinning like a zany and talking a blue streak. He was whistling in the dark. Trying to kid Tony out of it.

What the guy had done, I had no idea. But I had a pretty good idea where he was going.

My hands were clammy. It was hard to drive. What could I do? These guys were about to whack a guy. Right in front of me. I knew they were. And it was up to me to stop them. How could I do that? What was I supposed to do? Appeal to their better nature? Woodsman, spare that tree? Excuse me, sir, but have you considered the moral consequences of taking a person's life? Drive circles around them honking my horn till they realize it would be inconvenient to commit a murder with a lunatic around?

No. Alone and unarmed, there was only one way I could save this guy.

I whipped out my cell phone, dialed 911.

I was breaking my no-driving-while-dialing pledge, but 911 was only three numbers, and I didn't have to look. I punched them in, put the phone to my ear.

It rang three times.

Three times?

911 doesn't just pick up?

A woman said, "911, what's your emergency?"

"A man's about to be killed. An abandoned quarry in New Jersey."

"Slow down, sir. What was that again?"

"Two mobsters in a car, heading west, picked up a man in Manhattan and they're taking him for a ride."

"Is this some kind of joke?"

"We just came through the Lincoln Tunnel. The quarry's about five minutes ahead. Get the cops started. I don't know what road we're on, I'll give you the coordinates as soon as I can."

"Who am I speaking to?"

"That's not important right now. A man's

about to be killed."

"You're phoning an anonymous tip?"

I sure as hell was. The repercussions of the name Stanley Hastings appearing in the police roster would dork me geometrically.

"Come on, lady. Is this 911 or Facebook? Stop gabbing and send the cops."

It was a good retort, would have been better if I hadn't got cut off by a tractor-trailer and had to slam on the brakes and swerve to the left.

My cell phone fell from my hands, slipped down into the crack between the gearshift and the seat.

I couldn't tell if it was open or shut, whether it had disconnected 911, or still had them on the line. If so, they could hear me even though I couldn't hear them.

I rocketed by the eighteen-wheeler and spotted Tony's car up ahead. Thank God. I knew where they were going, I just wasn't sure where the turn was.

"They're still in sight," I said, for the benefit of the presumed, but by no means certain, 911 operator.

"Looks like he's slowing down. Think he's going to make a turn. Yes, he is!" I caught a street sign, shouted directions for the phone. "It's a couple of miles to the rock quarry, and I got no way to stop these guys, so you better hurry."

We whizzed by the stinking refineries, out through the flats, and took the turn into the quarry. I was still a coward's distance behind. Which wouldn't do. The cops weren't there. It was up to me to save the day.

How?

I slammed my car to a stop where I had before, bolted up the mound of dirt, just in time to see Tony and the driver walk the guy around the bend in the quarry out of sight. The guy walked ahead of them. Even from a distance he looked mighty damn reluctant.

There was nothing I could do. I was a witness, and that was it. I was drowning in self-loathing, inadequacy, and guilt. I watched, frozen, waited for the sound of the shot.

None came.

A silencer?

Tony and the driver came back out.

Trailing along behind was the guy. Alive. Just as Tony had done with his driver, they had gone in, looked, come out.

And were heading for their car.

Jesus Christ!

I had to get in mine!

I scrambled down the hill. Even as I reached my car, I heard the sound of theirs starting up. I'd taken too long. It was impossible to get out of the way before they appeared. They were going to find me, and kill me.

What the hell could I do?

I backed up, plowed the car into the bushes beside the road. Prayed there was no embankment, that there was solid ground underneath.

There was. I didn't go plunging into a river or smack into a tree. I went fully into the bushes until the first few snapped back into place, hiding the car. I killed the motor, hoped I'd been in time.

I had.

Tony's car rocketed by.

I waited a few moments, then pulled out of the brush.

Tony had a head start. It was going to be tough to catch him. I figured they were taking the guy back to New York.

But that was the least of my worries. If the 911 operator believed me at all, every cop in eastern New Jersey was about to descend on this quarry to prevent a murder. They would not be happy if I was the only one there. I had to leave, and fast.

The only thing was, I had to know: What was so all-fired important they had dragged this guy from Manhattan out here to see?

Cops or no cops, I had to risk it.

I started my car, pulled out, drove into the quarry. I stopped the car, got out, hurried around the bend.

I stopped short.

Looked at what the guy from Manhattan had seen.

It was a freshly dug grave.

56

My cell phone rang on the way back to New York. I fished it out from under the seat. It had fallen shut, severing my connection with the powers that be, but when I pulled over to answer, they were back.

"You called in an emergency?"

"Cancel the call. The incident is over, no one was killed."

"There was no emergency?"

"There appeared to be an emergency. Luckily, it was a false alarm."

"You turned in a false alarm?"

"No. I reported an emergency which gave every indication of being real. Luckily, it was only a warning."

"A warning?"

"Instead of hitting the guy they showed him a freshly dug grave, gave him every indication he was about to wind up in it. I would imagine it was very effective."

"So, you're saying there was no emergency?"

I hung up the phone. It rang again, almost immediately. I knew it would. I didn't answer.

I went through the Lincoln Tunnel, drove straight to the office building. Tony's car wasn't there. Of course it wasn't. It took time to pick him up, but it took no time at all to drop him off. They probably didn't even slow down.

I sat there, weighed my options. None looked good.

I drove to Westport. It's about an hour drive, but I needed time to calm down. I hunted up the post office, asked if they had a package for me. Damned if they didn't. I proved I was Stanley Hastings, and they handed it over.

I drove back to Manhattan, checked in with Richard. He wasn't pleased to see me. Of course, no one was these days.

"What the hell did you do now?" Richard said.

"I don't know. Why do you ask?"

"I just got a phone call. From the New Jersey police. Asking me to surrender you on a charge of filing a false report."

"Oh, for goodness' sakes."

"Apparently the cops are pretty hot about

338

it. I got a call from your wife, saying the same thing. According to her, you're not answering your cell phone. The cops can't reach you and your wife can't either and neither one's particularly happy."

"Richard —"

"Why, in the name of heaven, would you have filed a false police report?"

I told him. I can't say he was very sympathetic.

"You thought Tony Gallo was going to whack someone, so you called the police?"

"I couldn't just let him do it, could I?"

"I don't see why not. I mean, he was going to do it anyway, wasn't he? In your wildest dreams, was there some supercop who would magically appear and smite the gun from his hand?"

"Richard —"

"So, you called the cops, not to save this guy's life, but just so you wouldn't feel so guilty that you didn't."

"Yeah, yeah, I'm a bad person."

I set the package from the post office on his desk.

Richard eyed it suspiciously. "What is that?"

"Murder weapon. Weren't we asked to produce it?"

Richard rolled his eyes. "Wonderful. Now

you've got me concealing evidence."

"You're not concealing it. You're bringing it into court. In response to a *subpoena duces tecum.* What could be more legal?"

Richard opened his mouth, closed it again. "Actually, you're right. Well, that's something. A negligence lawyer with a murder weapon. I wonder if there's a precedent."

"So, that takes care of that," I said. "What about filing the false report?"

"Oh, don't worry about it. I can beat that easily."

"Because I didn't actually do it?'

"No, because you actually did. It's much easier to defend you from your actions. It's the stupid shit you blunder into that's a mess. What the hell were you doing following Tony Gallo?"

I told him my theory about Tony Gallo having a girlfriend, and MacAullif's theory about how I going about it wrong.

"I see," Richard said. "You thought that since it was MacAullif's theory and not yours, it wasn't necessarily bad."

"Yeah, but it is. What the hell difference does it make who the hell Tony Gallo's girlfriend is if it isn't one of the principles?"

"Yeah, suppose you follow him around for two days and find out he's seeing Susie

Creamcheese from Wilton, Delaware?"

"Wilton Delaware?"

"It's not going to prove a damn thing. Because it doesn't have a thing to do with the murder. Either murder. Because your ideas are going so far afield. Tony Gallo was at the motel. A dead guy was at the motel."

"You don't think following Tony Gallo is a good idea?"

"I think following Tony Gallo is probably not conducive to your health."

"So what should I do?"

"What should you do? Go to the movies. Take a walk in the park. Read a book. None of those things will screw up your life. Though, actually, you get a lot of bad ideas from books and movies. But do not, under any circumstances, tail any mafia dons."

"You got a better idea?"

"I *gave* you a better idea. I told you to follow the widow."

"I followed the widow."

"And you stopped at the police station, so you still don't know where she went. Which I pointed out to you, but did you listen? No. You decided to follow a mobster. And then blow the whistle on him for not whacking someone."

"You want me to follow the widow?"

Richard rolled his eyes. "I have a multi-

million-dollar law practice that is not depen-
dent on pro bono criminal work. I'd like to
keep you out of jail, but there are limits to
what I can do. Go and sin no more."

57

The widow sounded hassled. "Hello?"

"Hello, Mrs. Marston. It's Stanley Hastings."

"Who?"

Well, that was something. At least I wasn't uppermost in her thoughts.

"The private eye. You hired me. To follow your husband. Then you thought I killed him. Then you thought I didn't. I don't know what you think now."

"I have nothing to say to you."

"Yeah, you do. I was getting close to finding out what your husband was up to. Don't you want to know?"

"I don't have to talk to you."

"No, but you can listen."

Apparently, she couldn't. She hung up the phone.

Okay, best I could do without actually seeing her in person. And it was unlikely I'd get past the doorman this time. So the phone call was my best bet. It either worked or it didn't. I'd spend the day watching her apartment and absolutely nothing would happen and that would be that.

The most likely thing was that the widow would report me to the police. That's what she'd done the first time, that's what she'd do now. Only this time the odds were greatly increased that she'd phone. I could almost hear the cops saying to her last time, "Oh, you didn't have to come all the way," pressing business cards into her hands, telling her to call if that man annoyed her again. So, in all likelihood, she wasn't going to move.

I was so convinced of it I almost missed her when she did.

Her car came out of the garage, headed toward Madison Avenue, as it had to, it being a one-way street.

I fell all over myself sprinting inconspicuously for my car. If you've never sprinted inconspicuously, it's a knack. I reached Madison Avenue before she did, which of course meant that she had a wonderful opportunity to look through the windshield and see a crazy man running down the street. I hoped she wouldn't do that. I hoped she had other things on her mind. Of course, I'd just called her. I was the one prodding her. If she had any sense at all, she'd be looking out for me. Then again, as Richard, Alice, MacAullif, and nine out of ten doctors were sure to point out, she had to be nuts to hire me in the first place.

She went up Madison Avenue, through the park, and onto the West Side Highway.

If we were going back to the police station, it was going to freak me out. Although it would allow me to vindicate myself with Richard and do what I'd failed to do the first time: stake out the police station and see where she went when she left. And, sure enough, there she was, getting onto the George Washington Bridge.

I was a few cars back. I had to be a few cars back. Otherwise, I might as well have had my car painted shocking pink with the words DETECTIVE ON DUTY in orange, Day-Glo letters on the side.

From what I could see, the widow was taking no notice of her surroundings. She was, like last time, driving with a sense of purpose, full-speed ahead, within the limits of rush-hour traffic, but as far as I could tell, without a glance in the rear-view mirror. No, this woman knew where she was going and was determined to get there.

Why? What the hell was she doing? Didn't the cops give their cards? They couldn't be happy to see her again. This was getting to be a bad habit. She was becoming the widow who cried wolf. The cops would be getting less and less likely to listen. True, that one time her husband was dead, but she hadn't reported it.

At least as far as I knew she hadn't reported it. That started an interesting train of thought. She gets me out there with her dead husband and reports it.

Only that didn't happen. The motel manager reported it. Well, he claimed he didn't, but he was probably lying. Just like he was lying about the victim letting me in.

The motel manager. Another of the witnesses against me. They were adding up, the witnesses against me. There was Jersey Girl, who could attest to my impersonating an officer and appropriating a murder weapon.

I shuddered. That was the problem with thinking about this case. Every train of thought led to the fact that I was dorked.

Okay, lady. Enough idle speculation. Let's go to the police station.

We didn't. She breezed right on by the Ft. Lee exit.

My pulse quickened. We were heading for the New Jersey Turnpike. The widow was going to see Tony Gallo.

Wrong again. Instead of staying on Route 95, she took the exit for Route 4.

My mouth fell open.

The motel?

Could she be going to the motel?

That made no sense at all. Meeting her lover at the crime scene? I mean, Tony Gallo had to have brass balls, meeting the widow at the very motel where he killed her husband. Was it possible? A guy like that, maybe it gave him an added kick. But even so. The mind boggled.

She wasn't going to the motel. Disappointing, on the one hand, but bringing some semblance of sanity to the venture on the other.

So where was she going? Ikea? Yes, it's a shame Phil's dead, but now I can rid of that atrocious oak desk and get a nice breakfront. What a depressing thought. Tailing the widow on a shopping spree.

We didn't go to Ikea. The widow turned north on Route 17, offering other shopping opportunities too numerous to mention. I was quite familiar with the road. When Tommie was young, I used to take him to Sportsworld, let him play video games. Somehow I doubted if that was where we were heading.

We weren't.

The widow drove three miles north and turned into a motel.

58

So. Things had come full circle. Here I was, once again, staking out a motel. True, it wasn't the same motel, but you can't have everything.

The Double Pines Motel was fancier than the Route 4 Motel, but then anything would be. For one thing, it had more units. A lot more units. It was two stories high, and rather than having the office by the road with a dozen rooms stretching back in an L, it had a circular drive up to a central lobby, from which wings of units spread out in both directions parallel to the road.

The widow pulled into the circular drive, got out, and went into the lobby. She was back in minutes, hopped in her car, drove around, and parked in front of a unit.

I hoped hers was on the first floor. I don't know why I hoped that. It wasn't like I'd be looking in the window, or popping in the front door with a camera shouting, "Surprise!" Still, having her on the second story would, at least in my head, make the job harder. Of course, in my head, having her in a motel room made the job harder.

She took a unit on the first floor, cementing my opinion that it couldn't matter less if she did. I was also firmly convinced that, since I'd lucked out on the ground floor unit, something else would go wrong.

Nothing did. At least, not right away. The widow unlocked the door and went in, closing it behind her.

And there I was, once again, a private eye caught in a shaggy dog story, staking out a motel room, waiting to see who showed up. Only the first time, I had no idea a murder was involved. And the first time I had a client. And the first time I was getting paid.

There was one other difference.

The first time I had a Gatorade bottle.

I prayed it wouldn't matter. There was no reason why it should. No one checks into a motel room three hours ahead of their lover. If a lover was three hours late, the relationship wasn't going to last long. That was not the type of white-hot romance that would lead to the elimination of a spouse. No, the way I saw it, she called Tony Gallo the minute she hung up on me. And even if she called him at home, which wasn't likely, that would be a no-no considering the fangs on his wife, but even if she did, that would be an hour drive at best. No one drives slowly to a motel room assignation. One could expect a foot on the gas.

Except for rush-hour traffic. Good God, what if Tony got caught in rush-hour traffic? He could call the motel, ring her room, say he'd be late. And there he'd be, stuck in traffic, while I peed in my pants. Well, that would kind of put a damper on my denouement.

Stop it, I told myself. It's a long shot he's home in the first place. In all probability he's out scaring some poor son of a bitch to death with his freshly dug grave. He'd be along to get his rocks off and reassure the widow that no one was going to get them for murder if she just kept her head. Yeah, he'd be right there.

Only, if he were terrorizing another Manhattan businessman, he wouldn't bring him along. He'd have to take him back to New York.

No, he wouldn't. He'd have his chauffeur drop him at the motel and drive the guy back. And then go hang out in a nearby shopping mall waiting for the phone call to come pick him up.

Yeah, that's how it would work. And that's

how it must have worked with Vinnie Carbone. Which would have been just fine, because Tony Gallo wasn't boffing Vinnie Carbone's girlfriend, he was boffing the widow.

I took a breath. At long last, things were beginning to make sense.

Except how does the gun wind up with Jersey Girl?

Tony Gallo kills his chauffeur — bummer, now he has to drive himself, wonder if he ever learned — and now he's stuck with a murder weapon. So he lays it on Jersey Girl, who he must be boffing too, because otherwise how would he get so close? And why would his wife be freaking out? Though she could easily have made the same mistake as I, figuring Jersey Girl for the role that was rightfully the widow's.

It didn't matter. As far as I was concerned, I'd figured the motel murder out, in terms of who and why. At any moment, Tony Gallo's black sedan would drive up to the motel and everything would suddenly be clear.

Only it didn't. Nothing happened. Nothing at all.

Jesus Christ. How was this possible? No one checks into a New Jersey motel to be alone. But the widow did, and here I was, déjà vu, it *was* my first stakeout all over again.

Did the unit have a connecting door?

Was the widow dead?

No. There were no cars in front of the adjoining units.

But had there been when I drove in?

No. I was watching the unit, I would have noticed any comings and goings.

Or would I? I'd have noticed anybody *arriving*. But would I have noticed anybody *leaving*? From another unit, why would I? A car driving up could be pay dirt. A car driving away wouldn't mean anything. Would I have seen it?

Or what if Tony's driver dropped him off!

What if he was in there right now!

Was that possible?

No, it wasn't. I'd called the widow, stirred her up. She'd have called Tony. It would have taken him longer to get there than her.

Unless he was in the neighborhood. I knew he did business in the neighborhood, so if he was tooling around with his driver he could have had the guy drop him off.

No, not likely. For something like this he'd probably drive himself.

I glanced around the parking lot. At the far end of the lot, parked away from the motel, was a black sedan. Was it Tony's car?

I strained my eyes, checked the license. It was a Jersey plate, but I didn't recognize the number. I'd never checked the number when I was tailing Tony, because I'd already ID'd him. I'd seen it, but hadn't paid attention. Was it the same one? I didn't think so. But that didn't mean anything. That was the chauffeur's car. He probably had another car he drove himself.

I scribbled down the number. I could have MacAullif run it to see if it was Tony, but I'd kind of used up my favor quota for the moment.

It didn't matter. It was the only thing that made sense. It was his car, and he was in there.

All at once, the widow renting the downstairs unit was a great big plus. I hopped out of my car, hotfooted it up the driveway, and tiptoed across the parking lot, trying not to look like a private eye with a camera hoping to photograph a pair of illicit lovers in a motel room. Because that's exactly what I was. I had my trusty Canon hanging around my neck, over my shoulder, and down my side under my suit jacket, the way I smuggle it into the hospital to take injury photos of accident victims in bed. If they tried to leave before the cops got there, I was going to whip it out and start shooting.

I crept up to the unit, tried to peer through the window. No luck. The blinds had been carefully drawn. Well, that's an assumption on my part, but even if they'd been carelessly drawn they were doing their job.

I listened at the door.

Heard nothing.

Then a voice! A woman's voice! Talking to someone!

Unless she'd snapped. Unless it was all too much for her, and she was talking to herself. Because I, in my bumbling investigation, had driven her over the edge.

And then, like sonic manna from heaven, a low murmur came rumbling through the motel unit door.

A man's voice!

59

"You know an honest New Jersey cop?"

MacAullif snorted into the phone. "Is this a game?"

"Yeah, MacAullif. It's called Pin the Crime on the Perp."

"Is this the type of game where I wind up handing in my shield and my gun?"

"Only if you lose."

"What do I get if I win?"

"The charge of impersonating an officer goes away."

"I *am* an officer."

"See, it's working."

"I got a new case. You wanna stop screwing around and give me the gist?"

I did.

MacAullif listened, said, "Where are you?"

"Sitting on the motel."

"Promise you won't go in and find a corpse?"

"I won't go in. I doubt if he's gonna kill

her. It would be nice to catch 'em together, so it wouldn't be my word against his."

"Oh, was I dragging my feet? Sorry about that," MacAullif said, and hung up the phone.

I assumed he'd be sending cops. At least, I hoped that was why he'd hung up the phone. There were a number of other possibilities. In fact, hanging up on me was practically in his job description. Even so, I think he believed me. And if he believed me, he'd act. Whether it was quick enough to do me any good was another matter. But at least it wasn't a matter of stopping a murder. After my experience with the 911 operator, I'd had enough of life-or-death situations. Thank God this was simply sex.

Of course, the minute I thought that I started having doubts. It was only sex, but if this guy killed her husband, then she was the witness who could put him away. And this guy did not deal gently with witnesses. Look what happened to the chauffeur. All he'd done was rent the room. Not usually a capital crime, and yet he'd been put to death. In all probability, the guy didn't know anything except that the room had been rented. He might not have even known about the murder, known that there was any connection whatsoever. He might have been an unwitting accomplice. And still he bit the dust. So, was the widow really safe, when she knew everything that could put the guy away?

Sure she was. What, the guy kills her husband so he can have her, then he kills her? That didn't make sense. Well, maybe it didn't have to, if he was a full-fledged psychopath running on delusions of grandeur, as powerful men often are.

No, I was not considering walking up and banging on the door. I was standing unobtrusively beneath a tree growing on the narrow strip of grass between the parking lot and the road. I had a good angle on the door, and if the happy couple came out I was going to fire away. From a discreet distance. Not that I was afraid Tony Gallo would beat me up or kill me or both, but because I was afraid he would take my camera. While it occurred to me I might be able to outrun him, it also occurred to me I couldn't outrun a bullet.

Such negative thoughts were cascading with increasing intensity and frequency the longer the cops didn't show up. Where the hell were they?

I no sooner thought that but I was roused from my sordid musing by the arrival of the cops. At least it looked like the arrival of the cops, but it was only one car. That didn't seem right, somehow. I guess I was thinking of the movies, expecting SWAT teams to move in. This was just one car, and it wasn't necessarily going to the motel.

It was. It pulled in, drove right up to the unit.

The car door opened and the cop got out, and my heart sank.

It was Morgan.

Of all the cops in all of New Jersey, MacAullif has to get the one with the personal vendetta against me. Granted, a lot of New Jersey cops had reason to hate me lately, but, Jesus Christ, one of my arresting officers? Morgan, the guy who'd tricked me into a lineup when I thought I was going home.

Bad Cop's partner.

He wasn't going to make an arrest. He was probably sent here to look for me.

Morgan walked up and knocked on the door of the unit. Waited, and knocked again.

The door opened a crack. Then wider, and Morgan went in.

My head was coming off. What was going on here? Why was Morgan at the motel? There was only one thing I could think of: MacAullif had tried to get the Jersey Cops. Morgan heard about it. He raced out to the motel. Not to arrest the killer. To warn him. Because the cops had been in bed with Tony Gallo from the start. Which was the only thing that made sense. Which meant that I was utterly fucked, because now they'd just dig a big hole and climb into it and cover it up and I'd never get 'em. I'd be lucky not to take the fall myself.

Please, I begged. Don't let it happen. Let the other cops get there first.

They did. En masse. Just like in my fantasy. Local cops, state cops, and detectives in unmarked cars came screeching up, some with their lights on, some with sirens, some with both, skidding into the parking lot and squealing to a stop, forming a haphazard semicircle around the front of the unit. Cops pouring from their cars, streaming up to the door, forcing their way in. In less time than it takes to tell it, every cop in the state of New Jersey was in that motel room.

It was a good five minutes before they began filtering out. Some of the local cops first, uniformed cops, chatting with each other, leaning against their cars. No one was taking off. Now the arrest had been made, they were all hanging out to see the perp walk.

I understood the sentiment. I wanted to

see it myself.

Some of the state cops came out, along with a couple in plain clothes. The parking lot was filled with them.

Still no sign of Tony Gallo and the widow.

There was only one reason I could think of.

She was dead.

Any minute now, the EMS unit would come roaring up, medics would go in, realize there was nothing they could do, and call for the medical examiner.

The door opened again.

Bad Cop and Morgan came out with the widow. She was in handcuffs, but they seemed almost apologetic about it. Her hands were handcuffed in front of her, instead of behind her back. And they weren't yanking her by them. They were guiding her by the shoulders.

Bad Cop looked pissed. In the confusion, I hadn't even noticed he was there, but it was him all right, I could tell just from his expression, like he wanted to kill a PI.

The other cops gave way as they led the widow out.

And no one was paying any more attention to the motel unit.

I couldn't believe it.

Tony Gallo wasn't there!

My mouth fell open. I stepped out from underneath the tree, gawking.

Big mistake.

The widow's head snapped up. "It's him!" Being handcuffed, she had to raise both hands to point. "There he is!"

Bad Cop saw me. His face was murderous. For a moment I thought he might go for his gun. "Arrest that man!" he thundered.

I stood, frozen, while cops descended on me with handcuffs.

It occurred to me things couldn't get any worse.

Wrong again.

At that moment, Sergeant MacAullif came driving up to witness the arrest of Tony Gallo.

60

It was a zoo.

Everybody and his brother was in that courtroom — at least, everybody involved in the case.

To begin with, the judge was there, and an unhappier man it would be hard to find in the whole kingdom of New Jersey. As far as he was concerned, a simple murder case had escalated out of all proportion. Aside from having a massive mess to deal with, the poor man had to make sense of it all and render a decision that would not be reversed on the one hand, or make him look like a total fool on the other.

It was not the time to appear foolish, because the assembled multitude included several members of the media, not only newspaper reporters, but TV reporters as well. Cameras were allowed in the courtroom, a move the judge was probably reconsidering. I certainly hoped he would.

My ignominy was going to look bad enough in print.

I, of course, was the main participant. I was there with my attorney, Richard Rosenberg, to answer the charge of filing a false police report for the second time in two days. Being a habitual false police report filer was not going to look good on my record. Nor was the fact that in each instance I had falsely accused reputed mob boss Tony Gallo, a man unlikely to take kindly to such persecution.

Tony Gallo was in court with his attorney, primed to defend him in the event that I persisted in these charges, as well as to proceed against me if I did so. At least I certainly hoped he intended his attorney to proceed against me, rather than take matters into his own hands.

Also in court was the widow Marston and her attorney, not to answer the charges for which she had been arrested, which had been dropped, but to look out for her interests, much in the manner in which Tony Gallo's attorney was looking out for his.

Also in court was Jersey Girl herself, the other presumed mistress, and her attorney, an eager-looking young man, probably appearing pro bono, or at least on a contingency basis, in the event that a damage suit could be whipped up against yours truly, but more than likely seduced into appearing by the fantasies inspired by that amazing bod.

Also in court was Mrs. Tony Gallo, though whether to stand by her man or to substantiate yet another charge of impersonating a police officer was anybody's guess. She sat on one side of Tony Gallo, glaring daggers at Jersey Girl, who was not sitting on the other.

Also in court was Tony Gallo's driver, probably because he drove him there, but the way things were stacking up against me, I wouldn't have been surprised if he was there to testify that he had seen me spying on Tony Gallo's house.

Also in court was the motel manager, brought in no doubt to testify against me should the need arise. So far he had not noticed the presence of Sergeant MacAullif, who was doing his best to keep his face averted, and who was also there to answer a charge of filing a false police report. MacAullif had gone out on a limb calling the New Jersey cops for me, and it had come back to bite him in the ass.

MacAullif didn't have a lawyer, Richard having graciously volunteered to represent his interests, for which I was grateful. If the Truth be known, I was also grateful for the presence of the motel manager. Not wanting to be seen by him was probably the only thing keeping MacAullif from pushing Richard out of the way and tearing my head off.

Also in the courtroom were the prosecutor, two assistant prosecutors, the court reporter, the bailiff, and two court officers in addition to the ones guarding me.

Also in the courtroom was every cop in the state of New Jersey.

The prosecutor cleared his throat. "Your Honor, before we begin, I would like to point out that the defendant was served with a *subpoena duces tecum,* ordering him to bring into court the gun that he obtained from the witness, Angela Russo, by impersonating a police officer. May I ask if he's done so?"

"Oh, Your Honor," Richard said. "There are so many things wrong with the prosecutor's statement I don't know where to begin. He asks for the gun my client obtained by impersonating a police officer. No such gun exists. My client has *never* impersonated a police officer, therefore there *is* no gun that he obtained in that fashion, and we certainly cannot produce it."

The prosecutor put up his hand. "I concede that portion of my request may be stricken. Will you produce the gun?"

"I will certainly produce it at the proper time. I think if you will refer to the proceedings, you will find we were ordered to bring the gun in question into court at the defendant's probable cause hearing stemming from that charge."

"Your Honor," the prosecutor said in exasperation. "I have a ballistics expert here in court who is prepared to testify that the gun in question is the gun that killed Vinnie Carbone earlier this month."

"I don't care if it killed Osama Bin Laden. That doesn't alter your subpoena." Richard smiled. "However, the defense does not wish to be overly technical in so minor a matter." He pulled an evidence bag from his briefcase. "Here's your gun."

The prosecutor accepted the gun with poor grace. "Your Honor, I would like this marked for identification."

"So ordered. Now, could we get on with the task at hand? Let's proceed with the charges. Would the defendants please rise?"

MacAullif and I stood and faced the judge. At least, I faced the judge. MacAullif eyed the judge sideways while turning his head away from the direction of the motel manager.

"Stanley Hastings, charged with impersonating an officer, three counts."

"Your Honor," Richard objected. "The defendant has already been arraigned for impersonating a police officer."

"These are three extra counts, Your Honor," the prosecutor said.

The judge eyed him skeptically. "Separate counts?"

"Yes, Your Honor. Stemming from three separate incidents." The prosecutor continued, "Filing a false police report, two counts; conspiracy to file a false police report, one count; and Sergeant William MacAullif, filing a false police report and conspiracy to file a false police report, one count each."

"Your Honor," Richard said. "These charges are totally without foundation. I ask that they be dismissed."

"That is not the question, Mr. Rosenberg. How do the defendants plead?"

"Well, they certainly *intend* to plead not guilty, Your Honor, but I would like to know what they are pleading to. Just what specific crimes are they charged with?"

"Your Honor, the defendant, Stanley Hastings, has twice accused Mr. Tony Gallo, present here in court, of a crime. Once acting on his own accord, and once in concert with the defendant, Sergeant William MacAullif. In the former, he called nine-one-one to report that Tony Gallo was in the process of committing a murder. That charge not only proved to be false, but the defendant later admitted that it was false. We have the 911 operator here in court prepared to testify to that effect. In the second instance, the defendant conspired with Sergeant William MacAullif, of the New York police department, to accuse Mr. Tony Gallo of having murdered one Philip Marston because he was involved with Julie Marston, the decedent's wife. He named the widow, Julie Marston, as a co-conspirator and reported that the two were having a clandestine rendezvous at a New Jersey motel. The police responded to the scene and found Julie Marston occupying the motel unit alone. Nonetheless, they took her into custody for questioning. According to Julie Marston, the defendant had been pestering her at her apartment by phone calls and visits, and she had checked into a motel to get away from his harassment. However, this tactic did not work. The defendant followed her to the motel and conspired to file a false police report resulting in Julie Marston's arrest."

The prosecutor took a breath. "I realize

this is just a simple arraignment, but despite his exploits, the defendant has managed to stay released on bail. On the basis of this overwhelming offer of proof, I would ask that Your Honor rescind bail and bind the defendant over. In the case of Sergeant William MacAullif, who is a police officer, I have no objection to his being released on his own recognizance."

"Well, that's mighty nice of you," Richard said. "Do I understand correctly that if I don't object to you jailing one defendant, you will let the other defendant out?"

The judge banged the gavel. "That will do. We will have no such sparring between counsel. Mr. Rosenberg, personal sarcastic remarks aside, do you have anything to say to the prosecutor's charges?"

"I have plenty to say, Your Honor. As Your Honor no doubt knows, there are two defenses to a charge of filing a false report. Naturally, the charge can be defended should the report turn out to be true. If I can prove Tony Gallo guilty of the murder, you can't find my client guilty for saying so. But in the second case, in order to be guilty of filing a false police report, the defendant must have made the report *knowing it to be false.* Each report that my client filed he believed to be true. Since he believed it to be true, even if it turned out to be false, he is not to blame."

"He *admitted* it was false. I have the 911 operator."

"Which proves nothing. After the fact, he admitted he'd made a mistake. When he made the report he believed it to be true. That's all that matters. As soon as he realized he was in error, he said so."

"And has he admitted his error in accusing Tony Gallo of the murder of Philip Cranston?"

"In that instance, it is yet to be shown that he has made a mistake."

Tony Gallo's attorney, a beefy, well-fed individual, pulled himself to his feet. Compared to Richard Rosenberg, whose demeanor befitted a negligence lawyer, the man was a criminal lawyer, and showed it. "Your Honor, my client's not gonna sit here and be smeared. If the defendant keeps on slandering his good name, I'm gonna take legal action."

"That is certainly the thing to do. Settle the matter in civil court, not criminal. If we could proceed." The judge punctuated the remark with a harrumph. Then stopped as he noticed MacAullif's posture. "You there. The other defendant. Sergeant William MacAullif. You are a police officer. I would expect you to be familiar with proper courtroom decorum. Would you mind facing the bench, rather than favoring the court with your profile?"

MacAullif turned grudgingly, fighting for every inch.

There was an audible gasp from the other side of the courtroom.

The motel manager lunged to his feet, pointed his finger straight at MacAullif. "That's him! That's the man who came around asking questions!"

61

MacAullif was livid.

"If I lose my pension, I'm going to kill you."

"You're not going to lose your pension. Richard, tell him he's not going to lose his pension."

"I certainly hope not. He'll need it to pay my fee."

"I thought you were doing this pro bono," MacAullif protested.

Richard shrugged. "Filing a false report, sure. Impersonating an officer is something else."

"He's joking. Richard, tell him you're joking."

"He better be joking," MacAullif said. "If he's not, he's fired."

After the motel manager's surprise identification, court had taken a brief recess to sort everything out. MacAullif, Richard, and I were in a small conference room just outside the courtroom. There we no guards in the room, but two were stationed at the door, just in case anyone decided to take a hike.

"Your case is pro bono," Richard said. "How could I resist? It isn't every day you get to defend a police officer from a charge of impersonating a police officer."

"I'm thrilled for you," MacAullif said, dryly. "Can you make this charge go away?"

"Of course I can. For starters, I can probably ridicule the prosecutor so much he drops it. In any case, it's a piece of cake. The real problem is the false police report. Not that I can't beat it, but it's against Tony Gallo. It's not healthy to accuse Tony Gallo. *I* don't like accusing Tony Gallo, even on your behalf, and look at the position you put me in. To refute the charge, I have to show either that it's true, or that you had reason to believe it was true. In either case, I'll be saying things about Tony Gallo seldom said by anyone not subsequently found in the Hudson River tied to some concrete."

"But that's the charge you agreed to represent me on. Before this asshole ID'd me in court."

"I didn't say I wouldn't do it. I said it's a problem. You filed the police report based on something Stanley told you. Considering his record, that can hardly be considered prudent. At the very least, you would be guilty of reckless disregard."

"Thanks a lot," I said.

"So simply saying he told you so won't fly. You need some basis for thinking Tony Gallo was in that room."

"I still think he was in that room," I said.

"With a connecting door?" MacAullif said, sarcastically.

"What's wrong with that?"

"Two motels with connecting doors? I mean, once I can buy it. But you pull it a second time and my eyes glaze over. It's just an asshole theory. Even if it were true, he can't prove it."

"He doesn't have to prove it," I said. "He just has to raise an inference. Isn't that right, Richard? You just have to raise an inference?"

"Not against Tony Gallo!" MacAullif thundered. "You raise inferences against Tony Gallo, you are not long for this world."

"I quite agree," Richard said. "Nobody's going to prove Tony Gallo guilty. What we'll be trying to do is prove that there were reasonable grounds for you to suspect him, and that you did so with no malice of forethought. Continuing to hound him makes that difficult."

I snapped my fingers. "What if I could prove he was in that room?"

"What do you mean?"

I fished out my notebook, tore off the page on which I'd written the license number of the black sedan parked outside the motel, and handed it to MacAullif. "Here. Trace this plate."

MacAullif gave me a look as if I'd asked him to sacrifice his firstborn child. "A favor? Now you want a favor?"

"Don't be a schmuck. We're on the same side. This car was parked in the motel lot from the time I got there until the time the police arrived. If it's Tony Gallo's car, he was there."

"And it just happened to vanish into thin air?"

"You don't like the connecting door? Come on, we got nothing else. Just run the damn plate."

62

When court reconvened, the prosecutor rose to his feet. "Your Honor, in view of recent developments, I need to augment the charges against Sergeant William MacAullif. It now appears that he too is guilty of impersonating a police officer."

"Nonsense," Richard said. "He *is* a police officer."

"He isn't a New Jersey police officer."

"I'm not familiar with that charge. Impersonating a *New Jersey* police officer. That seems rather elitist. I thought that in the eyes of the law all police officers were created equal."

"You know what I mean. He pretended he was an officer involved in the case in order to glean information."

"An officer involved in the case. This gets better and better. Please, enlighten me. Which officer involved in the case did he impersonate?"

"Your Honor, this is not a laughing matter. It appears that Sergeant MacAullif, who has no jurisdiction in New Jersey, showed up at the motel and interrogated the manager."

"If Sergeant MacAullif, who has as much right to go to New Jersey as anybody else, chose to ask the motel manager about a crime that happened there, he was entirely within his rights to do so."

"But he represented himself as a police officer."

"He *is* a police officer."

"Don't start that again," the prosecutor snapped. "You know what I mean. He identified himself as a police officer and requested and obtained evidence in the case."

"What evidence?" the judge said.

"A photocopy of the credit card receipt of the man who rented the motel room."

"A photocopy of the victim's credit card?"

"Not the victim, Your Honor, but the man who rented the room next door."

"How is that possibly relevant?"

The prosecutor raised his voice. "Because the credit card belonged to Vinnie Carbone, who was himself subsequently killed by a .38-caliber revolver fired by the gun the defendant, Stanley Hastings, has just surrendered in court."

That announcement produced a huge re-action in the courtroom. The judge banged the gavel.

"Your Honor," Richard said, "I must object to the prosecutor's sneering in-nuendos."

"Do you dispute what he just said?"

"I dispute his interpretation of it."

"We're not arguing the case here. I'm ask-ing if this statement of fact is substantially correct."

"I fail to see how it is relevant."

"You think it's irrelevant that the defen-dant's alleged co-conspirator investigated and uncovered the name of the murder victim *prior to* the murder?" the prosecutor said. "Particularly in light of the fact that the defendant wound up with the murder weapon?"

Richard smiled. "He can't have it both ways, Your Honor. The prosecutor has already charged the defendant with imper-sonating an officer in order to obtain the gun in question from the witness, Angela Russo, after the body had been discovered. In light of which, the insinuation that he used it to kill Vinnie Carbone is absurd."

The court officer came through the gate, handed a folded piece of paper to MacAullif. He unfolded it. His face fell.

"A moment to confer with my client," Richard said. He sat down, whispered to MacAullif, "What's that?"

MacAullif shook his head. "It's no go."

He held up the paper.

I looked.

The car was registered to Sergeant Sam Fuller.

MacAullif jerked his thumb. "The ace detective here wrote down the license plate number of one of the cops."

"No, I didn't. This was before the cops got there."

"This was before you *saw* the cops get there. When you were following the widow, the cop was following you. The point is, it's not Tony Gallo, and we're screwed."

"Mr. Rosenberg," the judge prompted.

"Yes, Your Honor." Richard turned back to whisper again. "I think I'm going to have to consent to having you bound over."

"You can't do that."

"I have no choice."

Richard stood up, faced the judge.

My mouth fell open. "Oh, my God," I murmured.

Before Richard could make his motion, I grabbed him by the coattails, tugged him back down. Taken by surprise, Richard slipped, missed the chair, and fell to the floor, banging his head on the defense table on the way down.

63

Considering the indecorous nature of the interruption of the proceedings, Richard managed to maintain an air of formal dignity when court reconvened at the end of the five minute recess the judge allowed.

"Your Honor, I apologize for the unorthodox nature of the proceedings, but it has come to my attention that the defense has conclusive proof that Sergeant William MacAullif did not falsely accuse Tony Gallo of the crime of murder. Since the sergeant is a respected member of the New York City police force, I ask to be allowed to present such proof so that the charges against him may be dismissed. I will only need to call one witness present here in court. If that witness does not establish Sergeant MacAullif's innocence, I will withdraw my objection and consent to his being bound over."

"Does that go for the other defendant as

well?" the prosecutor asked.

"It does," Richard said. "If I cannot establish Sergeant MacAullif's innocence, you may rescind the defendant's bail and bind them both over."

"No objection, Your Honor," the prosecutor said.

"What witness do you wish to call?"

"Sergeant Samuel Fuller."

Sergeant Fuller took the stand and was sworn in.

"Your name is Sergeant Fuller?"

"That's right."

"You are a member of the major crimes unit?"

"That's right. And if you think I'm going to perjure myself for the defendant just because I'm a cop and cops stick together, think again. I don't know the defendant and I don't know why he did what he did, but I'm certainly not going to stick up for him."

"You don't know the defendant Sergeant MacAullif?"

"That's right."

"But you do know the defendant Stanley Hastings?"

"I ought to. I arrested him enough."

"And when was the first time you arrested him?"

"At the Route 4 Motel, when I arrested

him for the murder of Philip Cranston."

"Are you acquainted with Mr. Tony Gallo?"

"I'm a police officer. I have met him in the course of my job."

"But you have no personal relationship?"

"With Tony Gallo? Certainly not." Sergeant Fuller put up his hand defensively. "No offense meant, Mr. Gallo."

"Let me ask you this. Are you acquainted with Angela Russo?"

"No, I am not."

"Really?" Richard said. "Didn't you call on her after the murder of her boyfriend, Vinnie Carbone, and question her about her personal involvement in his death?"

Fuller glanced over to where Jersey Girl sat among the witnesses. She looked quite voluptuous in a yellow scoop-neck pullover. "Oh, that's what you meant. I thought you meant know her socially. I don't know her, but I did question her."

"Really? You're from Ft. Lee, she's from the Jersey Shore. Isn't that a little out of your area?"

"I'm with Major Crimes. We have a wide latitude."

"Uh huh. And while you were questioning her, did you plant the gun used to kill her boyfriend in her apartment?'

Sergeant Fuller's mouth fell open. "I most certainly did not."

"Really? Didn't you and Tony Gallo decide she was becoming a liability, just like Vinnie Carbone had become a liability, so you framed her with the gun? She knows you did. At least, if she thinks about it. She didn't find the gun until after you were there. She didn't think anything about it, because it was Vinnie's gun; she figured he just left it there. But now that it's been identified as the murder weapon, she knows he didn't leave it there, and she didn't kill him, so the only way it could have got there —"

Jersey Girl sprang up, boobs a-bobbing. "That's exactly what you did!" she screamed, and launched herself across the courtroom.

Mrs. Tony Gallo met her halfway, and the two women fell to the floor, punching, kicking, and gouging at each other as the courtroom went wild.

64

It was easy after that.

Since I was the only one who had the faintest idea what happened, Richard was able to negotiate immunity for me and MacAullif from anything short of murder, in exchange for my story. This was only slightly unnerving, since I was making it up as I went along, and with murder still on the table, it wasn't as if the prosecution didn't have recourse.

The epiphany for me was the realization that the widow Marston was having an affair with Sergeant Fuller, not Tony Gallo. Once I realized that, everything fell into place. I hound the widow, and she goes right to the police station. Not to report me — she's having an affair with a cop.

And how did Tony Gallo disappear from a motel room surrounded by police? *He was never there*. The widow was there with Sergeant Fuller. He was there when she got there. His car was parked inconspicuously at the far end the lot. I wrote down the license number. When MacAullif called the cops to sell them on the idea that Tony Gallo killed a Manhattan businessman and was having a tryst with the widow in a New Jersey motel, Morgan got wind of it. He hightailed it to the motel, banged on the door, pushed his way in, and told Sergeant Fuller to get dressed and get a pair of handcuffs on the widow so when the cops showed up they could lead her out. That's why I never saw Sergeant Fuller arrive. I thought I just missed him. But he was already there. He was there and Tony Gallo wasn't, and that's where I made my mistake.

Not that Tony Gallo was innocent. Tony Gallo was in it up to his eyebrows. Which answered another question. Why does a mob boss from the Jersey Shore drive all the way to Ft. Lee to have his meetings? Because he's in bed with the local cops. Because there's a Don't Ask Don't Tell motel with a connecting door where he can meet anyone he wants without having to be seen entering the room. In the course of the last few years, he had used it many times.

Alice put her finger on it, not surprisingly, with the question I couldn't answer, "Why did the widow hire you?" That was the key to the whole thing. The widow hired me because she was setting up her husband to be murdered. She wanted a credulous PI to follow her husband to a motel, stake it out, and be prepared to testify that no one, least of all her, went near the place when the guy was killed. Which would have worked perfectly if Tony Gallo's name hadn't come into it.

I followed Marston to the motel, hoping to get a picture of the bimbo he was cheating on his wife with. Only there was no such woman. Marston was mixed up with Tony Gallo, and he went to the motel to meet him. Tony's in the other room, just as he is for business meetings, only this time he comes through the connecting door and shoots Philip Marston dead. This is partly as a favor for Sergeant Fuller, who's got the hots for the widow, and partly because Philip Marston has proven deficient as a business partner, and Tony Gallo does not take kindly to reversals of fortune. Tony kills him, wipes the gun clean, leaves it under the bed, goes back to his unit and checks out. I actually saw him leave, but I never would have connected it if I hadn't seen him in another context.

Meanwhile, Bad Cop and Morgan are hanging out in the police station, waiting for the 911 call reporting the crime. It comes in, not from the motel manager, but from Tony Gallo himself, phoning in an anonymous tip. They saddle up and ride out, just in time to catch me in the act.

The motel manager was innocent, by the way. At least the way he tells it, and frankly I don't think he was bright enough to make it up. But according to him, he didn't call Tony Gallo and tip him off that MacAullif was nosing around the motel register. His story, which was too absurd not to be true, was that after MacAullif left, he called the police station to report that the dumb cop they sent to get a credit card receipt from the crime scene made a mistake and got one from the room next door.

Which was a red flag for Bad Cop and Morgan. They immediately checked, saw that Vinnie Carbone had signed the receipt in question in his own name. Which made him a huge liability. Vinnie Carbone was just a driver, he had no idea why he'd rented the room, he did it all the time. He wasn't even aware of the murder, but if questioned he would spill the beans.

So Vinnie Carbone had to go. Bad Cop called on him at home, ascertained that he was indeed as stupid and dangerous as they thought. So Fuller feeds him some bullshit story along the lines of if he's going to be driving Tony at night, he's gotta have a gun. Vinnie shows it to him, and Fuller picks it up and shoots him dead.

Fuller hangs onto the gun till he can plant it where it will do the most good. I probably would have been first choice, except he is not eager to connect the two murders together.

When Fuller tells Tony Gallo what happened, Tony has an idea. He's been having a fling with Vinnie's girlfriend, Angela Russo, and lately she's been making a pest of herself in a way that's roused the suspicions of his wife. So Tony figures to kill two birds with one stone. As soon as the body's found and the investigation begins, Fuller calls on Jersey Girl, questions her about her boyfriend, and manages to plant the gun in her apartment. Where it undoubtedly would have been found by the police after sufficient time had elapsed so she wouldn't connect the gun to his visit.

Then I step in, impersonate a police officer — for which I have immunity, thank you very much — appropriate the gun, get it tested, and proceed to have a nervous breakdown.

Jersey Girl had no inkling the gun was the one that killed her boyfriend. Or that Bad

Cop was the one that pulled the trigger. But once Richard confronted him in court, she realized what he'd done. He'd been in her apartment and he'd planted the gun. Vinnie's gun. He'd taken it, and he'd killed Vinnie with it, and he'd planted it on her. That realization transformed her into a vengeful tigress. I think she would have torn his eyes out right on the witness stand if Mrs. Gallo hadn't intervened.

And Bad Cop really was a bad cop. I suppose that shouldn't have surprised me as much as it did. But sometimes the simple explanation turns out to be true. Even if it happens to be mine.

So things worked out. Bad Cop and Tony Gallo got indicted for the two murders — in each instance, one as the primary and the other as an accessory before and after the fact. Their lawyers should make a hell of a lot of money, and probably won't do them any good. The widow Marston lucked out, if one can call it that, and only got indicted for the murder of her husband. And much as I hate to kick a widow when she's down, Richard volunteered to sue her for my fee.

As for Jersey Girl, I guess she went back to teasing hair and tantalizing men. She hadn't done anything wrong, unless you count boffing a mobster or lying to a police officer, of which she was actually innocent, since the supposed police officer was me. And her only real lie was that her boyfriend had given her the gun. She found it in her apartment and assumed she had just over-looked it, though she was sure she hadn't. Which is probably why she accused me of planting it. It had to be in the back of her mind. She actually had the right explanation, she just had the wrong perpetrator. When she saw I wasn't going for it, she lied and said Vinnie gave her the gun. Which would have meant she was guilty of murder, if I believed it. Lucky for her, I didn't.

As for the good guys, I got off the hook for murder, MacAullif got off the hook for filing a false police report, impersonating an officer, and choosing his friends unwisely, and Richard got his twenty-five grand back. Kind of a win-win all around.

Once things got straightened out, I called Mike Sallingsworth in Atlantic City to tell the ex-PI he was off the hook. Turned out he didn't need to be told.

"So, Tony Gallo went down," Mike said.

"How you'd hear that?"

"I keep track of people who could hurt me. His name's high on the list."

"I didn't lead him to you."

"Doesn't matter. You came around asking questions. Tony Gallo was the answer. I didn't give it to you, but that would be small consolation if he got it in his head I did."

"I wouldn't worry about it. Trust me, Tony Gallo's going to be doing serious time."

"Maybe so, but guys like that got a long reach. You might want to have someone start your car for you for a while."

I shuddered. "Thanks. That hadn't occurred to me. Now it will be all I think about."

"You're really not cut out for this business, are you?" Sallingsworth said. "You ever think about retiring?"

"I need the money."

"Don't we all."

Later that night I told Alice what Mike said. About retiring, not about starting my car.

She didn't say I couldn't, or that we needed the money, or what else could I do, or anything of the kind. All she said was, "You're not that old."

I found that disturbing on so many levels.

Anyway, I'm not about to retire.

But after careful consideration, I've come to the conclusion that stakeouts are possibly a little beyond my area of expertise.

I should probably try to stick to trip-and-falls.

ABOUT THE AUTHOR

Parnell Hall is an Edgar, Shamus, and Lefty nominee, and is the author of the Stanley Hastings private eye novels, the Puzzle Lady crossword puzzle mystery series, and the Steve Winslow courtroom dramas. An actor, screenwriter, and former private investigator, Hall lives in New York City.

The employees of Thorndike Press hope you have enjoyed this Large Print book. All our Thorndike, Wheeler, and Kennebec Large Print titles are designed for easy reading, and all our books are made to last. Other Thorndike Press Large Print books are available at your library, through selected bookstores, or directly from us.

For information about titles, please call:
    (800) 223-1244

or visit our Web site at:
    http://gale.cengage.com/thorndike

To share your comments, please write:
    Publisher
    Thorndike Press
    10 Water St., Suite 310
    Waterville, ME 04901